Sermon of the Mount

Sermon of the Mount

First published in Indonesian under the title *Khotbah di atas Bukit*
by PT Dunia Pustaka Jaya, Jakarta, 1976
Copyright to the English translation © 2018 Joan Suyenaga
Copyright to this edition © 2018 The Lontar Foundation
All rights reserved

Funding for the translation of this book was provided by
the Indonesian Translation Funding Program
of the Ministry of Education and Culture, the Republic of Indonesia.

Template design by DesignLab; layout and cover by Cyprianus Jaya Napiun
Cover illustration detail from *Red Line* by Djirna, 1995.
Image from the book *Indonesian Odyssey* courtesy of Equinox Publishing.

ISBN No. 978-602-9144-41-3

MODERN LIBRARY OF INDONESIA

KUNTOWIJOYO

Sermon of the Mount
a novel

translated by
Joan Suyenaga

Jakarta, Indonesia

1

Actually, old Barman liked having a companion like Poppy. He would call to her, "Poppy dear!" Then the young woman with the exquisite body would come, kiss him, and say, "You're cold, poor thing." She would tell him to drink a glass of wine, which would warm his body and set it on fire and then, before his eyes, she would transform into a ravishing creature, arousing him. He would drink the mixture of honey and egg that his lover provided for him, while she prepared their bed in the mountain cottage, where he would be lulled to sleep by hopes of incomparable happiness. His gray hair, wrinkles, and creaky old bones meant nothing once the woman lay down on the bed. He was seventy-six years old, and her smooth, fragrant, shapely body belonged to him.

He had to share her only with the cold nights, which made him jealous. He would drown in a deep sea, grope in its depths, its entirety. A miracle! At that moment he would envision his Poppy with her eyes closed, moaning, begging him. And then he would recall—although it wasn't there—the extraordinary fragrance of the jasmine blossom. He would wrestle with his aged body until he was exhausted and he would always end up saying, "I'm sorry, dear." He would kiss Poppy, and she would gaze at him vacantly. Oh, poor old Barman! Poppy would lie on the bed, bitterness buried deep within, stunned to see her golden body unused. If she didn't feel sorry for him, she would have lashed out at him in frustration.

Then after she regained her composure, she would kiss him coldly: "It's okay, papa." She would try to smile as if she had forgotten her unhappiness. "Ah, my Poppy. You're my beautiful doll." His head would spin; he wouldn't sleep all night, thinking about the woman lying beside him. It had happened countless times.

According to Bobby, Barman's son, Poppy was the perfect woman to be his companion throughout his retirement and perhaps for the rest of his life. Bobby thought that if his father lived on the mountain with a woman, then his life would be perfect.

"You may be able to live alone in the city, Dad, but it would be impossible on the mountain," his son said.

Bobby had come to him one day with an intriguing idea. It was a bit impertinent, but Barman knew what he meant.

"Why do you want to spend the rest of your life in the city? Take a vacation. Take a trip to the mountain. After all, we have a house on the mountain, don't we, Dad?"

At first, Barman rejected the idea. Why would he go to the mountain to escape loneliness? He was living in the midst of thundering printing presses and the screams of his grandchildren. How could he be lonely in the city? He could ask for anything from his daughter-in-law. If he said, "Dosy, I want a cold drink," then cold water or orange juice would quickly appear on his table. He could take his grandchildren for a walk, buy them candy, and watch them chase each other around. He could stroll in the city in the evening with the black umbrella he'd bought in Paris and pretend he was walking in some European city. It was pleasant enough. Why would he want a vacation house on the mountain? He wanted to dote on his grandchildren as a grandfather should. He did long for a quiet place on the mountain, but that didn't mean that he wanted solitude!

"Ah, you won't be lonely there," Bobby said.

Indeed, Barman's doctor had once recommended that he live in a quiet, cool place: the mountains. So his son had bought a vacation house there.

"It's for you, Dad. Just for you," his son said.

Barman had even tried to stay there one night, and at the time he dreamt about living there forever. But to really do it? He would have to think about it again. Would he enjoy the solitude?

His son laughed when he heard that question.

"Ah, as if I wasn't your son, Dad…"

Bobby suggested that his father have a companion.

He said, "I know just the person who will make the time fly. Time will fly by so quickly, you won't realize the passing of the day."

Barman's aged blood boiled as if it was popping through his veins. Warmth seeped throughout his body and he was pleased.

"All right, show her to me, son. But don't tell Dosy."

Bobby brought a woman with a perfect body to his father. Barman's old eyes bulged when he saw her. The woman remained calm.

As if he were dropping the card on the table, he nodded. "Agreed."

This was the woman who would attend to him in his old age. To return the favor to his son, he was asked to recite a few sentences—he didn't care what they meant—and sign some papers in the presence of some officials. He did it all without thinking. *If the woman did not ask for any guarantees, what were the papers for? They didn't need a contract.* The woman agreed to everything, as if she really wanted to do it for herself and not for either Bobby or Barman.

"Good-bye, Papa!" "Good-by, Grandpa!" said Dosy and her children.

Barman's daughter-in-law had packed everything, because Bobby had planned his father's departure for what he envisioned as "voluntary and complete tranquility." Barman would have the chance to enjoy complete rest without being pestered by his grandchildren. They sent him off as if they were never going to see him again, but with touching cheerfulness. Barman saw the tears in his daughter-in-law's eyes, but he didn't let it bother him. There was nothing odd or awkward. Everything went smoothly, no one was coerced. The woman who had just joined them seemed to be happy. Her laugh was even merrier than Dosy's.

Indeed, at one point Barman had heard Dosy arguing with Bobby.

"You're making a mistake, Bob," Dosy had said.

"I know my father better than you do, Dos. Be quiet, this is better for him. What's more, the doctor agreed to this plan."

"But Papa is so old."

Bobby laughed. That argument did not change anything.

It was Bobby who had searched for a female companion for Barman. He'd shown several photos to his father. All of them pleased Barman's seasoned good taste in women.

Bobby pointed to one of them. "This one is dark but sweet, Dad."

Barman just smiled as he watched his son. Barman knew about women. In the past, he would joke that he always "knew what a woman was like just from her photo." Now he could see himself in Bobby.

"This woman is very smart, Dad. Slender, tall, fair," said Bobby pointing at another photo. "And she has decided to be faithful to only one man. One man."

Barman peered at the black-and-white photo and tried to imagine the color of the woman's skin, the fullness of her body, her height and carriage. Then he asked to see her in person.

"Ah, you're clever. I think she's the best one. Her name is Poppy."

Poppy. It was a name that had a familiar ring to it. He felt as if he had known it for a long time.

"Poppy," he said. "That's a very pretty name."

Children play with dolls, but old Barman would play with a living, warm-bodied human being. A living doll, solid and warm. "My dear Poppy." The name took on a new meaning for him. At the end of his life he could call out a name that excited him, that would raise his spirits. What could be better for him than the warmth of a woman in the chilly mountains? He would have a new purpose for living. It would be like a long, weary journey that ended with a refreshing rest. He could imagine how he would shiver in the mountains without a woman by his side. But with Poppy there, the flowers in the yard would be more fragrant, the grass would be greener. *It will be sweet all day long! Tra la la!* He wanted to sing when he heard the hum of the car that was to take him to the mountain. Good-bye commotion! Good-bye chaos!

Barman liked women. When his wife died, Bobby was still flying kites. Every day during the windy season Bobby would ask, "Dad, let's get kite string." Barman would go along with his son's wishes and buy the kite string. He had spent the cold winters in France with Bobby—and only Bobby—vacationing in Cannes. He had never given his adorable son a stepmother. Barman did not want to upset his son, so he never remarried. Bobby lived with his father, a diplomat, throughout the bright days of their life abroad. Now that little boy had given him grandchildren.

The son now knew what he should do for his father. "Dad, this is the woman," Bobby said.

Years ago, during a vacation, Bobby found his father making love to a blond woman. Barman quickly said, "Bob, consider her your mother." Bobby asked in Indonesian who the woman was. When she asked Barman what the child had said, he replied, "Ah, he is a good boy, *ma cherie*."

Barman often gazed at a picture of Bobby's mother and showed his son how much he still thought about his deceased wife. "This is your mother, son." He even told the woman he'd brought to his room, "This is my love—my wife." The picture of the dark woman that hung on the wall was never disturbed, no matter what happened. Barman took it with him from place to place wherever he moved throughout his diplomatic career. He became used to saying: "This is a picture of my wife, my dear. Don't be angry, but I still truly love her. Come, let's dance."

Before leaving for the mountain, there were many things to do at home and Bobby was busy making arrangements for the move. There was a small party at home to welcome Poppy. Dosy, it turned out, could be a wonderful hostess. Old Barman was rather embarrassed when his children and grandchildren raised their glasses and shouted, "For our two grandparents!" He glanced at Poppy. She was calm. She smiled and raised her glass. In a moment, he lost any feeling of awkwardness. He soon forgot about the party that night. He didn't know why, but he did not want to think any longer. He wanted his life to be a kind of heaven that perhaps he might not enjoy for long. The party turned out to be a bit of a torture for him. Bobby wisely called an early end to the party.

"Enjoy your time there, Dad."

Everything was ready: house, flower garden, yard, kitchen, and view! He would enjoy the mist that gathered around his feet. At night, in the distance: the twinkling lights of the village, sparkling fireflies. Then he would close the bedroom door, push aside the clean mosquito net and soak up the sight of the warm white bed and Poppy!

The trip to the mountain was a lovely dream, like something he had never experienced. Barman asked the driver to slow down, and he tried chatting with Poppy.

"It's beautiful, Poppy, that road we just passed. Look at the red flowers there!"

The woman smiled, gazing in the direction that he pointed, wiping the glass window so that that she could get a better view. Barman watched her curved fingertips rest briefly on the glass, her painted fingernails, deep red-orange.

"And there, Poppy, we'll climb to that peak there some day! Our cottage is behind that cluster of trees."

He could envision his bed, but he didn't mention that to Poppy during the journey. They laughed together. Actually, the old man had not imagined that it would be that easy for her to converse with him. Whenever he had a chance to steal a glance at her, he would shiver and think: *Ah, a doll as ravishing as this! But you're such an old man, Barman.*

This thought had once snuck into his dreams of passion. He had consulted a doctor about overcoming the limitations of his old age. The doctor had advised him to get a woman, just one woman. Had the doctor informed Bobby of this? *Ah, my Bobby.* His son had ordered him to go to the mountain and had made arrangements for this trip, this "trip to heaven." The mountain of hope. He thought of the old phrase, "expectations as high as a mountain." *Would that please Poppy?*

Barman did not want to talk about anything except the journey itself. As someone who has spent a lot of time with women, he knew how to save or postpone a topic of interest. Someone anticipating the chill of the mountain—he forgot whether it was Bobby or he himself—had packed a coat for him and a woman. He took out the yellow coat.

"Here's a coat for you, Poppy."

He draped the coat on Poppy's shoulders, touching her arm lightly.

"No, thank you, Papa. I'm not cold."

"You're not cold?"

He thought: *Ah, your body is warm!* He could feel the heat of the woman's body. *Thank goodness, Poppy, you don't need a coat.* He liked healthy women. The ideal combination: the sophistication of the city and the healthiness of the mountain. He suspected that Poppy was this kind of woman. Barman was pleased.

The mountain road was still misty in the morning.

"That's our cottage, Poppy, covered with mist. From a distance it looks dark, but as soon as we reach it, you'll see that it's as clear as it is here."

Just then, he wanted to see the view. He ordered the car to stop and they got out. He took out a pair of binoculars from his bag and offered them to Poppy.

"Look, it's great, isn't it? You won't find a view like this anywhere else. Even in the Alps."

Poppy looked out at the panorama and said, "It's wonderful, Papa. Where is our house?"

Barman searched for it in the greenery.

"It's behind those trees, Poppy."

"And that, Papa, what is that red color in the valley?"

"Flowers, Poppy. It's flowers!"

A breeze blew under Poppy's skirt. He was like a child who had just seen something wonderful. Momentarily stunned, he swallowed hard. He thought: *Could he still do it?* Quickly, he returned to the car, pulling the woman's hand.

"It's chilly," he said.

The car continued up the mountain, green grass lining the road. Barman watched Poppy as the car continued to climb.

When they reached the cottage, Barman opened the car door quickly.

"Leave the things there, Poppy. Let's look around. This is our first day!"

He held Poppy's hand so tightly that she felt as if she was being dragged. She complained briefly then smiled and followed him.

"Where are we going, Papa?"

"For a walk, Poppy. The view in the morning is great. Out here, in the middle of nature. Come on, Poppy."

They ran, holding hands. Poppy laughed too. It was a magical moment in the undergrowth, a joyful chase, surrounded by shady trees and shrubs. Soon the laughter subsided, followed by a secretive silence. The wind blew through the trees, carrying a long sigh from the underbrush.

They returned to the house and hurried indoors. Barman threw himself on the sofa. The woman approached him, ruffling his white hair.

"Ah, Papa. Look at your hair."

His hair was full of pine needles. The old man opened his eyes and closed them again, wanting to will away the exhaustion that had just overpowered him.

"I want to sleep a bit, dear."

The woman placed his coat over him. They were like an old couple.

"Do you want a drink, Papa? What would you like?"

The woman found the kitchen and busied herself settling in. The morning passed. The mist evaporated, leaving them in sunlight. Everything was crystal clear, the peak of the mountain, the valley, the trees, everything. There was light everywhere, even in the undergrowth, which had become an enchanted forest!

The driver had brought all of the bags and boxes into the house and then left. Now they were alone in the isolated cottage, without a car and far away from everything. Bobby was right when he said it was "perfect isolation," but it was pleasant.

There were houses scattered across the side of the mountain. From a distance, they looked like small mounds of earth. Nestled in early morning sunlight, the hillside awoke. From his cottage, old Barman began to enjoy the view of the rough edges of the garden, lined with overgrown grass and shrubs, bathed in the morning light. The journey had taken only an hour, but he felt that they were very far from the city. This world of old Barman and young, beautiful Poppy.

When Barman woke up he was embarrassed that he had fallen asleep in Poppy's lap.

"What time is it?"

He felt refreshed so he decided to telephone his son to report their arrival.

"I'm very happy, Bob."

Barman wondered why he felt so refreshed. *It must be because of Poppy. Where was she? Ah, she was coming to him. Light, bright footsteps. What kind of lover was she? What was her body like? Ah, here she was!*

"Papa, have something to drink," she said.

She held a cup in her hand.

"You must be very tired, Papa."

What kind of drink was this? He stretched out his hand, took the cup and smelled: honey and egg.

"You're so good to me," he said.

Just at this moment he started to feel young again. He emptied the cup.

"You mixed in some pepper, didn't you?"

Warmth spread from his mouth to his throat, down to his chest. Poppy had retreated back beyond the doorway. He sat gazing at the empty cup on the table. Drops of the brown liquid slid slowly down the side of the cup, forming a shallow pool in the saucer. He watched it for a long time. He felt warm so he removed his coat. He realized that the back of the coat was dirty and he remembered how he had rolled in the grass with Poppy that morning. The memory upset him, so he tried to dismiss it. Poppy returned and helped him to fold the coat.

"Your coat is dirty, Papa."

Again, he remembered Poppy lying in the undergrowth.

"Look, here, it's dry grass." Her fingers flicked the grass off the coat.

"These are pine needles." He reached out to touch Poppy's hand. "You're a naughty woman, Poppy!"

She pulled Barman's hand.

"Remember, Papa. Only a naughty woman can please a man."

Barman wanted to continue the banter, so he held on to her hand. Poppy tried to pull away.

"Patience, Papa. There's still tomorrow."

She took his cup away. Her fragrance lingered behind and Barman inhaled deeply, trying to keep the woman with him.

Poppy was quick. She shouted from the other room, "Dust! How can there be so much dust flying about on the top of a mountain like this? Papa, I'll have to clean the rooms first before we can sleep."

It was actually Barman's fault that Poppy had to clean the rooms before they could sleep there. He hadn't wanted anyone else to live in the cottage. No one. He had said that he would clean it himself with his own hands but, of course, Poppy was better at that than he was.

There had been a caretaker at the cottage before Bobby bought it, but Barman didn't want to waste money on a caretaker, so the man was dismissed. The house on the mountain was locked up. *What was there to worry about? No wonder there was dust everywhere.*

Poppy burst out again, "How can it be this bad?"

Poppy had difficulty with the vacuum cleaner because there was a problem with the electrical sockets. *Ah, these villagers*, joked Barman. He set up the machine and showed her how to use it. He knew Poppy was clever—at least for practical handiwork—and she quickly mastered the use of the machine.

Bobby had once said to his father, "Dad, if a person lived alone in this cottage, he could cook anything easily."

Anyone with enough energy to breathe could live here. Living was easy! Barman was pleased to know that he wouldn't hear any complaints such as: Where's the oil? or Oh, the stove doesn't work! No, there wouldn't be any complaints like that. The days would be filled with purposeful laziness. There would be free time to play around.

Barman showed Poppy how to use the kitchen appliances. And the knives! There were many kinds of knives here. Bobby had stored away in this house all the kitchen utensils he had brought from Europe. Dosy had said once that the house was perfect in every way. Barman added in his mind: *Yes, and with the addition of a beautiful woman named Poppy, this house is paradise.*

He had already shown Poppy how he'd like her to make his coffee.

"Put the sugar and coffee in here, add water and then milk. Stir it and let it settle for fifteen minutes, and then it's ready to drink."

Poppy didn't mind being treated as if she were stupid and had to be taught how to do things. Occasionally Barman called her a "village girl," then added "but young and pretty." He liked women who took pride in themselves. In just one day they had become close, inseparable. They were equally responsible for the easy rapport. Barman hadn't thought it would be so easy to be comfortable with her, but it seemed that it was all right for the old man to be paired with such a young, pretty woman. He was overjoyed that it took only one day for their relationship to settle comfortably. He felt confident.

That evening he paced back and forth.

He asked, "Have you heated the water for my bath, dear?"

Earlier he had told Poppy that he didn't dare bathe unless there was hot water.

"Ah, grumpy old man," said Poppy with a light cheerful tone, which made him think that this was a woman who was born to serve men, to make them happy.

"Take a bath and scrub well. I'll get you some milk. We'll eat later after the sunset, okay, Papa?"

He was proud of his beloved Poppy.

He was pleased that even as an old man he still could enjoy life with a beautiful woman at his side. This was really how he should live out his later years. If the story of his life was ever written—perhaps by one of his grandchildren—they should focus on the last part of his life. Happiness could be achieved on a mountaintop. He had spent his free time that afternoon observing his Poppy—how she walked, how she moved, how her slippers sounded, even how she breathed. Sometimes when she caught him gazing at her, he would chuckle. Poppy smiled—she was always smiling—and he was struck by the way that she showed her beauty. After catching her eye, he plopped down again in a chair. Her smile lingered in the corner of her eye, as if it was eternally present deep in her soft brown eyes. As he sat in the chair, he wondered what she was doing. *Ah, she's here with me.* He was embarrassed to admit that he was infatuated with her.

At the same time he felt stupid. Why didn't he tell her not to do any housework and just sit with him in the living room? He restrained his longing to stay in the kitchen with Poppy. Men should not chase women. Would he dare make any suggestions? He wanted to show Poppy the bare peak of the mountain, the valleys and massive boulders.

The thought occurred to him as she happened to be passing by, and he asked hesitantly, "Did you know, my dear, the peak of the mountain is beautiful in the evening?"

That was one way, the most refined way, to invite her to take a walk.

She glanced at him.

"Your eyes are as clear as spring water," he said.

"Just a moment, Papa."

Yes, of course, she had to prepare dinner. He regretted that Dosy had not sent them their meals as well. This irritated him. *A pretty woman should be loved, not drowned in kitchen work.* His anger spilled forth. He slammed the nearest door: Crash! The slam surprised him. *What a crude thing to do!* He stood at the door, hoping that Poppy didn't hear it. He wanted to ask for her forgiveness, so he pushed against the kitchen door, but then he didn't know what to say.

Hesitantly, he mumbled, "I think it was the door."

"That's okay, Papa"

How patient that woman was! She immediately forgave him. Relieved, old Barman returned to the living room. He gazed out at the green grass and flowers scattered everywhere shimmering in the last rays of sunlight.

Barman was proud of his considerable experience with women and achieving the heights of perfection with them. Quietly, he was pleased with his life. He had lived and worked in the most beautiful places in Europe. He always felt that to know the women of a country was to know the country itself, and vice versa.

When he and Bobby had returned to their homeland, they decided to settle in the city that was best for business. Bobby had fulfilled his dreams. They bought printing presses, and at first the roar of the machines was very pleasing for Barman. When Bobby was able to run the company by himself, Barman left the business. He was getting old. He called the machines "stupid and boring." He began to enjoy exploring the city, where everything looked strange, new and intriguing. He often invited his young grandchildren to join him on his walks. His youngest grandchild entertained him with a ringing squeal, "Grandpa, candy!" Barman got to know the city quickly, and soon he felt that there was nothing new in the city anymore. It was exactly like what he had seen in the printing house: nothing but machines.

He had once said, rather timidly, to the mayor, who he had met through other important people in the city: "Your city is dead. It's filled with nothing but soulless three-dimensional objects!" Although he was not interested in philosophy, he thought he could explain what he meant. The mayor just shrugged his shoulders, and that made old Barman sad.

After that encounter, Barman began to feel like a stranger in the city—that it wasn't the place for him anymore. He felt alone even though he was in the middle of bustling activity. Who would pay any attention to an old man in the midst of all that commotion? But it wasn't just that that made him feel lonely. It was a feeling that he could not explain—that he had lost something or that he was on a journey that would never end. Sometimes, when he wandered in the city, he felt as if he were pacing the sidewalks of Amsterdam or Paris or Haarlem. He no longer invited his grandchildren to join him on his walks, even though they begged to tag along. Dosy would tell the children, "Grandpa's going out just for a short while and later he'll bring you some candy, okay?"

Once, Bobby entered his room and asked him, "Dad, tell me… What is it that you want?" His son had watched him get thinner by the day. Even Barman did not know what he wanted. *Did he still want something? What was lacking in his life? Was he beginning to feel his age? Was this ageing process leading to his death? Wouldn't everyone's heart stop beating at some point? He wanted something!*

He thought about it for a long time as he looked at Bobby, then he shook his head slowly. "I don't know, son."

Bobby took him to the doctor for an examination.

The doctor reported, "Your father is as healthy as a horse, Bob."

He was relieved to hear that.

Then the doctor continued, "But it would be better if your father lived in a cooler climate. The tropical weather is not too kind to him."

This would mean exile! Barman rejected this piece of advice. Initially, Bobby also refused; he wanted his father near to him. But the doctor convinced him, and one day the loving son brought his father a picture of a cottage in the mountains.

"Dad, this is a gift for you."

A house with a grassy backyard. A house in the mountains. He took Barman to visit the place immediately. Barman fell in love with the house.

"I'm going to figure out a way so that you can be comfortable here," said Bobby.

When Barman decided to live in the mountain house, he took a farewell walk around the city. He walked all day. Bobby had to ask his driver to search throughout the city for his father. The driver found Barman sitting alone in the city park, gazing forlornly at the people passing by. Barman was glad to leave his old world. As he was returning home with the driver, he swore, "To hell with the stupid city!"

Poppy's voice rang out clearly, "Papa, papa!"

He rushed to the kitchen.

"Try this. Taste this. Is the seasoning okay?"

It was delicious, divinely delicious! Even his wife—Bobby's mother—had never cooked anything as good as this, even though he always tried to correct her. He had often complained, "Where's the salt?" But now he praised the cook. Not just because she was his beloved companion.

"You're a good cook, dear."

Poppy smiled. "It's for you, Papa," she said.

You-you-you. He looked at her hair, her nose, her throat, her shoulders. His body stirred. He held Poppy's hand.

"Ah, this hand can cook well, too, can't it?"

He tried to hide his passion. He thought: *In a little while, the sun will set.* He recalled what had happened with Poppy in the grass that morning. It was embarrassing! It wasn't a good idea to rush anything. He had stopped before anything had happened. He returned to the living room, looking forward to the evening.

Poppy had demonstrated her remarkable talents as a homemaker. What did she say when she served Barman at lunch earlier? "Have more, Papa." And he added more food onto his plate. "Have more meat, Papa." Even though she had not cooked the lunch, Barman pretended she had. Dosy had packed food for their lunch. Poppy said that she would cook the evening meal. He thought, "grains of rice as white as pearls" in gratitude for Poppy's service. But he was careful and did not want to risk her laughing at him, so he just said, "The rice, tsk, tsk, so white. And warm. And served by a beautiful woman!" How pleased he was!

After lunch Poppy had said to him, "Papa, you can take a nap now." How brazen! He suspected that this was a *fait accompli.* Actually, he longed to take a walk. The tangerine tree in the yard was laden with ripe fruit, waiting to be harvested. Poppy did not realize this.

It would be so restful to sit beneath the trees in the afternoon. He would tell his beloved, "This is my paradise." The promised land. There was nowhere else on earth Barman wanted to be than here on this mountain: that's how happy he was. It was so different from the busy, dusty city. Life felt settled on the mountain, as if suffering would never find its way there. Barman tried to erase from his memories the bustle of the city and everything that had happened there. If he had known about the beauty of the mountain, he would have chosen to come here earlier. True happiness had come late to him. His only regret was that he was so late in discovering the beauty of this place. *Would this be his final home? Was this a solution for his distress?* Damn! He had just been daydreaming of taking a walk with Poppy beneath the trees when she had told him to take a nap.

He was not interested in sleeping just then. He didn't feel any need for a nap.

He said, "There's no reason to take a nap, Poppy."

"That you are old is a good enough reason."

Hmph, the woman was pressuring him. He had never been able to forgive laziness, but coming to this mountain was all about being lazy. *All right, he would retreat to the bedroom, but to take a nap by himself when he had a lover would be torture. Dictator!* His beloved led him by his hand to the bedroom. Like a naughty child, he tried to resist—but, of course, he was just pretending. He trembled as he held Poppy's hand. When he sat down on the bed, he tried to reach out for the row of buttons on his beloved's blouse. She giggled, then she vanished into another room.

He heard Poppy complain from the other room, "Oh, this house is a dust trap! I'll have to clean up before doing anything else!"

Barman lay back on the bed, releasing his disappointment, consoling himself: *Of course, this house should be cleaned. Curses!* But in a short while, he had forgiven her. Poppy worked hard that day. She prepared dinner. Before falling asleep, just to sneak one more glimpse of his beloved, he went to the kitchen and said, "Boil water for my evening bath."

Barman wanted to telephone his son to tell him about the situation with Poppy. He wanted to complain about Poppy's cooking duties. *It's an old formula. The man falls in love through his stomach. It really is true that delicious food is like the devil.* As he picked up the telephone receiver, he heard noise in the kitchen again. *What was she doing now? He didn't need a housewife; he needed a lover.*

"Oh, is this Dosy? Yes, tell Bobby that I am very happy."

Dosy asked him about the weather. Was it good or bad? Were the flowers wilting or blooming? He told her that everything was pleasing to his eyes and he didn't care whether the weather was good or bad. Everything was good because Poppy was there. But when the conversation was over, he regretted that he might have implied that he was not happy living with his grandchildren, whereas, in fact, they had delighted him. Let it be. He returned to his room and quickly fell fast asleep.

After he woke up and bathed with warm water, he headed for the terrace. The last rays of the sun softly touched the crimson flowers and green grass in the garden. The colors shimmered in the evening glow. A slow breeze rustled through the leaves. He could hear something—a gentle whisper of pine needles or a waterfall in the distance. When he was in the bathroom, he remembered that he had wanted to take a walk. He splashed water over his body while mumbling the lyrics of a song that he couldn't quite remember the words for. In the end, he just shouted, "My Poppy, my sweet one, *ma cherie*, my dear…"

He became uneasy as he waited on the terrace. *Where is my Poppy? She isn't here yet even though I told her we were going for a walk this evening. The sun goes down quickly on this mountain. It would be a pity to waste this chance for an evening walk.* Traces of sunlight were still in the sky, a wash of pale yellow and white. The pastel colors would soon be replaced by deepening red. Then he saw Poppy! She was in the middle of the flower garden. He rubbed his eyes. It was true. Quickly, he headed for the garden.

"A woman and a flower. Two beings of equal beauty," he said.

She turned to him, smiling. He stood at the edge of the garden enjoying the view. Poppy was standing among the flowers, his angel in the Garden of Eden. Aware of being in the midst of nature, his gaze floated to another part of the mountain. Magnificent Nature. *And this is its beautiful enclave*, he thought—the valleys shaded with the long black shadows of towering trees and the sun, golden red.

He said, "Look at the sun, Poppy. Some people don't like the mountains. Tell me—who is as stupid as that?"

Barman picked a flower and walked carefully towards Poppy, avoiding the rose bushes.

He gazed for a long time at a spray of violet flowers, then said, "These are the most beautiful of all the flowers. What are they?"

He knew they were some kind of orchid. Poppy said they were orchids. When she approached him to look at the flower, Barman stepped back and said, "Look, I love you both!"

Poppy stood up on her toes and kissed the old man's cheek. Barman was ecstatic.

"Naughty grandfather," teased Poppy.

Barman laughed.

"Spoiled girl," he replied. *The girl is mine*, he thought.

"Come, let's explore our new world," invited Barman.

Poppy stretched out her hand, and they took turns leading each other around the garden. The exploration was even more amazing for Barman because he was holding Poppy's hand. It was a happiness he had never experienced anywhere, whether it was with his deceased wife or with any of the other women he had been with, too numerous to count.

"Listen, Poppy. I feel as if I've been born again. Right here."

Poppy welcomed the statement by tightening her grip on his hand.

"Yes, that's how I feel too, Papa."

"How do you feel?"

"Exactly like you do. I feel as if I have been born again."

"Why do you feel that way, Poppy?"

"I've made a complete cut from my past. I'm a totally different person from the one I have been. And it's not just a feeling. My thoughts and my actions are really new. I have made a conscious decision to live like this, Papa."

It was a long statement. It was not that important for Barman to understand Poppy. It was enough that she served him. What was important now was what Poppy was doing for him, not what she was doing for herself. Everyone took care of himself. It was egotistical, of course. He was pleased that Poppy wanted to give him everything.

"Are you willing to give me everything?"

"Of course, Papa. That is what I have decided."

They walked across the grass.

Barman said, "This grass is the carpet promised in paradise, Poppy. It can be found only on this mountain. Not in the past, not in the future. Only now."

"You don't believe in heaven?"

Barman only laughed.

"This is paradise, I hope." He continued, "It doesn't matter. If it exists, then thank goodness, but if it doesn't, then that's okay."

Poppy did not respond.

Barman concluded, "If there is a paradise, then surely it is something like this. I cannot imagine a place more like what I hope for than what is here right now."

"I hope it's really like that, Papa."

Barman did not know very much about this woman. Actually, he preferred to look after himself. Because of his experiences and beliefs, he had not paid much attention to women, except for sex because that part of life could not be tended to alone. This woman gave him hope, because just looking at her raised his spirits. He had high expectations of her. What he needed was the skin and body of a woman, not her feelings or thoughts. He knew about love, but did that have to mean that the person he loved would be less free to be herself? Let Poppy feel whatever she was feeling. Now, the sun was taking its leave. The grandeur of Nature in the evening with rays of fading sunlight touching Poppy's skin stirred his desire to savor her body.

A bat flew past signaling the arrival of night. The evening sun colored the sky. Herons from distant rice paddies below flew past them in a V-shaped formation. It was wonderful to be out in nature as the sky began to darken.

Barman pointed to the birds.

"Poppy, look! Where are the birds' footprints?"

Poppy laughed, thinking that it was just a riddle.

"Where?" repeated Barman.

"There aren't any," said Poppy.

"That is what our lives are like. No traces left. Gone. Who knows where? Unknown."

They reached the edge of a cliff. There was a valley far below them. A gust of wind blew beneath Poppy's skirt.

"Oh, this wind!" complained Poppy.

"Ah, it's as if we were flying, isn't it, Poppy?"

Another flock of herons passed near them.

Barman began to speak. "Poppy," he said, "Just like you, I want to leave my past behind. Just as the birds don't leave any tracks. No tracks at all. That's what I mean."

The sun left the day behind.

"They always look forward. Not back. History is taboo for them; the past is past. But is that enough, Poppy?"

They were silent.

"If you don't want to continue with this conversation, just say so. Perhaps you're bored."

The red deepened in the sky and it began to cool down. A mumbling chorus of animal sounds rose from the undergrowth. Another gust of wind whipped up.

"Let's go back, all right?" Poppy stretched out her hand.

Barman complained. "Why?"

"It's embarrassing. We always return to the past. We go out and come home again."

They returned to the house as the pine trees blended into the fading green background of the hills.

When they reached the door, Barman asked, "Why do we always return?"

Poppy was busy flicking off the dry grass that had stuck to the hem of her skirt.

"This skirt is too long."

Barman looked at the skirt and her two fair feet. The day had turned to night, and there were those two fair feet!

Bobby telephoned to say a belated "good evening" to his father. He asked whether his father was comfortable in the new house. *Happiness, son, complete happiness.* Bobby asked if he could speak to Poppy. Barman told his son to wait because Poppy was in the kitchen.

"Poppy, auntie. Don't let my father think, okay?" said Bobby over the phone.

Poppy didn't understand what he meant.

"I mean, don't let him think about anything. About work or anything else. He must forget that he is a thinking creature."

Before Poppy replaced the telephone receiver, Barman wanted to speak to his son again.

"Yes, this is a very special evening, Bob. Have you ever seen herons line up and head for their nests? ... What? I don't have to think? Ah, you're just joking. We're different from them, Bob. Good night!"

The cottage was a bright light in the midst of the darkness. The mountain was quiet, waiting for the night and for sleep. There were lights on part of the mountain. Electrical lines stretching up the side of the mountain helped relieve the darkness of the night. Small flying creatures swarmed around the lights. Mist swirled around the electricity poles. The swarming insects disrupted the dense mist, creating what looked like clumps of cotton hanging from the electric lights.

Barman finished everything that evening. Eating, sitting. He no longer read. The cupboards were filled only with clothes. He didn't have any papers or writing implements. Papers were part of his past. Now he wanted to start something new. When he was born he had nothing, not even thoughts. He wanted life to be as pure as it was when he was born. Barman hoped he would find that pure life on the mountain. He had taken down all the pictures that his son had hung in the cottage. He would start life again like everyone at the beginning of life, naked and searching. He felt honored with that decision. He did not tell anyone about this, not even his son Bobby. He had made a decision and then forgotten that he had decided anything. Everything started and ended with himself.

Poppy was now in the same house and the same room with him. She was ready now. She did not have to work in the kitchen at night.

Poppy asked him, "Should I turn off the light, Papa?"

"Just leave the corner light on."

So Poppy turned on the dim light in the corner and turned off the light in the middle of the room. The room darkened, setting the atmosphere for his desires. Barman did not yet know much about Poppy. He had not had a chance to ask Bobby or Dosy about her. He wanted to live in the present and for tomorrow morning! Poppy was Poppy, the woman who was now ready to sleep beside him. Barman was worried that he was too old for this young woman. His forehead was lined, his body weak, and his veins protruding. Meanwhile, there was Poppy, so young and fresh!

"I want to talk a while before sleeping, my dear."

To his surprise, Poppy rose from the bed and moved to the chair. She sat down.

"Papa, that's not usual for me. There's no use in talking about anything. Sleep, yes, sleep. Besides, I was told to make sure that you didn't think."

Barman laughed. He immediately forgave her. He got up from the bed, and stroked her hair.

"My dear," he said softly, as if only the night could hear him.

Ah, poor old Barman! He remembered the doctor and Bobby. They went back to bed and Poppy fell asleep. He knew that the woman would regret that he was so weak. *Indeed, I'm so old, Poppy. Why did you come here? Who told you to come here? Bobby! Why you? What is he hoping for?*

After he had regained some strength, he returned to the living room and left Poppy alone. He suspected that the woman had fallen into a deep sleep. He was worried. He remembered his doctor who had said, "Try it, just try it."

Now he had tried and failed. Again. It reminded him of walking alone in the midst of the city, alienated and powerless. That same feeling had arisen again. *Oh, yes, as when he was a child and he liked to hunt for birds in the mountains.* The night was chilly.

Poppy called out, "Papa, where are you?"

She came looking for him in the living room.

"Come to sleep, Papa!"

Barman looked at her.

"I'm sorry, Poppy," he said. "Maybe I'm too old."

"Ah, Papa. Have faith! No man is too old for any girl."

Barman knew that was Poppy's way of comforting him. *Did he still have to be humored like that?* Poppy held his hand tightly.

"Go to sleep, Papa. Don't think about it anymore."

Barman obeyed, he closed his eyes. He was trying not to think about anything and to go to sleep. *Was he real? Or was he just a symbol of his anxiety?* He questioned his existence. Wondering if perhaps he indeed did not exist, Barman fell asleep. It was a black night, under a black sky, beneath black trees.

2

Barman was sorry for Poppy because of all the kitchen work. True, she was very docile and domestic, but he couldn't understand why the work in the kitchen took so much of her time. He never knew when she woke up in the morning. It was only after the room had warmed up, more because of the electric lights than the sun, that he got up and found that everything had already been prepared for him. Morning on the mountain was always wrapped in mist. Shades of green mixed with milky white mist that hung loosely on the leaves, lacing around the tips of trees, knolls, and the roof of the house. Barman wanted to explore his surroundings after his warm morning bath. He rubbed his body vigorously and wrapped himself in warm clothing. Just for once, he wanted to capture the beauty of the morning. He had asked Poppy to wake him, but it seemed that she preferred to let him sleep until he woke up by himself. He could not blame her, of course. As he poured warm water over his body, he thought: *This is one of the pleasures of old age.*

Both Dosy and Poppy took good care of him and he was equally fond of both of them, but it was only with Poppy that Barman could tremble with anticipation. His new life was filled with unfamiliar feelings. Feelings that were foreign, strange, but exciting. It had been a long time since he had shared a room with a woman who would do anything for him without asking for anything in return. Although he often wondered about Poppy's behavior, he did not intend to ask her about it. He also hoped that Poppy would not ask him anything about himself. Knowledge was not always useful. So when he poured water over his head, he felt as if he was cleansing himself of his past, even of his knowledge. *This warm water is the neutralizer for knowledge and life's stories. History enchains us! Go to hell!*

He wanted to be at peace with the mist, the grass, the trees, the hillocks, the overgrowth, and the chill of the mountains. At peace with nature, with every greeting he uttered. That was why he left Poppy in the kitchen before eating and went out to greet the morning. "Poppy is a true homemaker," he said as he strolled through the garden with his hands in his pockets. He pulled up the neck of his jacket and let the morning breeze play with his white hair. He whistled, perhaps because of the bitter tea and bit of bread he just had. He took tentative steps through the grass as dewdrops splattered the bottoms of his trousers. Although his shoes were damp, his shirt and rain jacket kept him warm.

The panorama was new for him. Traces of sunlight penetrated the mist. He liked walking in the mist, imagining himself drowning in the mysteries of nature, envisioning a distant world. *Is this our life?*

Houses were scattered across the mountainside. There were many houses and perhaps many people who lived in them. But they were all still hiding in their houses. Barman did not feel it was necessary to seek out new friends. He preferred to be by himself, in fact, alone in the densest mist, as if he would always be safely at a distance from everything. Birds flew low, their feathers damp, flapping their wings. Barman shouted wildly when, in the thick mist, a bird swooped so low that it grazed his head. He swore, "Damn you!" and then laughed. He felt close to nature. He thought that he was being reborn in nature. He would postpone any impulse to meet people. As much as it was possible, he would avoid going to the market, unless, of course, Poppy wanted him to go with her. He should have brought a fishing pole! He could see a streak of white in the distance. It must be a river. He liked to walk. A yellow-feathered bird flew by and perched in a tree. He headed towards the tree, whistling, until the bird flew away. *Ah, the bird did not know that I am now one of its kind, an element of primeval nature.* He tried to follow the yellow bird's flight, but it was absorbed into the mist. He stood there for a long time. *This is my world. That bird is just like me!*

Barman was not aware that a man with a cane was standing behind him. The man had stopped; he was watching Barman. The stranger touched Barman's shoulder, but he did not turn around.

"Hey, what are you doing?" said the man.

This is strange, thought Barman. *This has never happened before. Who's talking?*

The stranger was patient. The two men resembled each other very closely. The only difference between them was their clothing. Other than that, they were exactly the same.

"I'm looking at a portrait of myself," mumbled the stranger.

Barman turned around and immediately the stranger ran away. Barman chased after him. Running unsteadily, he shouted, "Hey! What did you say?"

Barman quickly ran out of breath. "Hey, stop! There's no use in running, friend."

The stranger stopped in the distance and leaned on his cane. "Good morning," he said.

"Who are you?" Barman asked.

"I am the guardian of this mountain."

As if in a dream, Barman watched as the stranger was swallowed up again in the vegetation. He was perplexed by the strange encounter. The stranger had nimbly avoided him. Barman thought: *Perhaps it was a rabbit.* He gazed in the direction where the stranger disappeared, but he could not see anything anymore. *Ah, just forget that a stranger or some creature came to you, Barman.* He rubbed his eyes and tried to dismiss the incident. He looked at his watch. *Oh dear! I've been out here for a long time. Poppy is surely waiting.* He turned back towards the cottage that was now bathed in sunlight, surrounded by green grass and the roses blooming in the garden. *A paradise of flowers*, thought Barman. He picked out the thorns that clung to his clothes while murmuring, *ah, ah.* The pricking thorns aroused him.

He could see Poppy from his vantage point behind the flower bushes. She was standing behind the glass door. Perhaps she was looking out for Barman. Aware that he was being observed, the old man stroked his cheek, his wrinkles. Poppy was wearing a pink dress. Barman tried to avoid the woman's gaze by crouching behind the flowering bushes. He recalled the sounds he heard in the forest when he was young.

He called out clearly, "Lu-lu-lu! Lu-lu-lu!"

He continued to call, hoping that Poppy would come out when she heard the sound.

"Lu-lu-lu!"

He was right. Slowly and gracefully like a goddess, Poppy opened the door and stood in the doorway. *It's not good for a girl to stand in the doorway in the morning, Poppy.* When she began to walk out onto the grass, Barman watched how Poppy's pink dress contrasted with the green grass. *She's like a blossoming fresh flower moving slowly amidst its leaves!* The sun and Poppy both shone equally brightly to his ageing eyes. He pinched the stem of a flower so that it swayed as if something was hiding beneath it. His trousers were damp from the grass and prickly with thorns. *Ah, these thorns!* He heard a soft clear voice.

"Papa, Papa!"

The gentle voice touched his ear. More than the twitter of birds in the trees, he felt this voice deep in his heart. He liked this game.

Again, he called out, "Lu-lu-lu!"

Poppy was approaching, so he crawled slowly in another direction. The leaves rustled, his shoes stuck in the earth and several thorns scratched him. His skin itched, so he stopped to scratch it. A thread from his shirt trailed behind. A yellow leaf fell from the top of a tree and tickled his neck. He flicked it aside.

Suddenly Poppy was standing beside him. He could smell her perfume mixed with the fragrance of the flowers. She brushed aside the leaves that covered him. From his crouching position, Barman could clearly see Poppy's legs, feet, and sandals. He was thrilled with the sight. *Such beautiful feet!* He closed his eyes. *What an exciting game!* He wanted to touch her feet. He reached out to touch her legs when Poppy pulled him up by his shoulders.

"Come on in, you'll get cold," she said.

Barman stood up, brushing the dirt from the bottom of his trousers. They stood together amongst the flowers. Barman, intensely aware of their presence in the garden, smiled at everything around him.

"What are you doing here, Papa?"

"Waiting for you, Poppy. Standing here, here in the flower garden!"

"What are you looking for here?"

What am I looking for? Beauty! Eternity! Goodness! But wait! He repeated the question in his heart. Poppy was leading him away. Apparently, the woman did not need a reply. *She's right. We don't need anything here. Just to live. And nothing will happen.* Barman did not want to leave the garden immediately. He pulled away from Poppy's hand.

"No, no."

She tightened her grip and grasped Barman's elbow. He had to acknowledge how strong she was.

"Your clothes, Papa. They're dirty!"

Barman gave in. The woman tidied him up. She flicked off
the dirt from his clothes and squeezed out that parts that were
damp. Her hand felt soft on Barman's skin. When she led him
out of the flower garden, he followed. Being obedient occasionally
was pleasant, too. Barman looked up to the sky, and to the lights
shining in the distance. *Here they were, together, in the midst of
nature, on this mountain.*

He remembered once again the direction in which the stranger
had vanished.

"What are you looking at?"

He didn't want to tell Poppy about the stranger, so he said, "A
rabbit."

This was a version of a truth, because he had called the stranger
a rabbit.

"I like rabbit meat," said Poppy.

"I'll find one for you some time, my dear. There are many wild
rabbits here."

"They're tasty, a bit like chicken."

"Now I'm hungry. We haven't eaten yet."

They headed for the house holding hands. Barman asked what
she had prepared for breakfast. He asked if Poppy preferred a savory
or sweet breakfast. They could eat whatever she wanted. Poppy said
that she would eat anything. Then she said that Barman should tell
her what he liked.

Poppy would be busy with housework. Her work was endless. It
would be hopeless to invite Poppy out for a walk in the mountain
countryside, so Barman considered leaving her at home. He felt
sorry for her tender feet. Walking about in the mountains was not
suitable for beautiful feet. An indoor woman like Poppy would
not endure climbing over mountain rocks. Surely she would
complain as they walked, "Papa, my feet hurt." He did not like to
hear complaints like that. It would disrupt his plan. Poppy already

loyally prepared his meals and bed. That was enough, more than enough for an old man like himself. He had seen the neighbors' houses in the distance. No, he didn't want to meet his neighbors. He just wanted to see the houses as part of the view. From the knoll in his garden, he had seen the red rooftops of the houses below and the white walls of the houses above. Actually, he only wanted to meet the stranger who had appeared that morning. That is, he would be pleased if he did meet him. Otherwise, he did not want to disturb his solitude. His well-intentioned solitude.

He prepared his cane, hat, and shoes. They were perfect for mountain walks. He stomped as hard as he could on the floor to make sure they were sturdy. He felt warmed by the food that Poppy had served—spicy pepper soup. Poppy knew that Barman was preparing to go out.

"Papa, tell me. When are you going to take me for a walk around this mountain?"

Barman mumbled a reply while tightening his shoelaces.

"Hiking is for men, Poppy."

"All right. We'll have a breathing contest."

Barman again felt the age difference. *Perhaps Poppy was stronger than he was. Ah, no. Women were indeed weak.*

Then, Barman thought, *Oh no! She was beginning to whine. Would he have to follow her wishes? It was Bobby who suggested that she be his companion. She's as strong as a horse! The view will be beautiful with that woman at your side, Barman. Ah, that would be true if we were not on a mountain. The woman would have difficulty hiking in the mountains.*

"Hiking is not good for women, Poppy."

"But I like it."

"I'm going for a long walk."

"Where?"

"See that speck of blue? I'm going over there." He tried to tighten his shoelaces. Poppy knelt down to help him.

"It's so far!" said Poppy. "You won't get back by evening."

Poppy had finished helping him tie his shoelaces. When she stood up, Barman held her chin and kissed her.

"Believe me, I will return, my dear."

Quickly, the man picked up his cane and hat. "I'll see you later," he said.

Poppy walked with him to the terrace. When she lost sight of him behind the overgrown grass, she returned into the house. She sat in a chair in the living room, gazing out the windows to the distant sky and the floating clouds. She sat there for a long time, unaware that her eyes were wet and that several tears had fallen into her lap. She wiped her eyes and tried to sing. A bird flew by, then tried to fly through the glass, but was struck down. After a moment, it revived and flew off.

Barman tried to remember in which direction the stranger had gone. If he found him, Barman would call the man "Mr. Rabbit." Only rabbits come and go so easily in the overgrown grass. The sun warmed his body. He hoped that he would meet someone who would perhaps become his friend. He wasn't sure. Initially, he had not wanted to meet anyone during his stay on the mountain, but the stranger this morning intrigued him. His old feet stepped nimbly through the grass. His feet felt light, as if he were going to a party. He was pleased that the houses on the mountain were far apart and separated by hills and valleys. The mountain air was invigorating, and the alternating heat of the sun and the chill of the mountain air pleased him. The fresh air and the sun's warmth slowly spread throughout his body. There was a bit of a breeze. To his left and right, the overgrowth was unkempt, but sprinkled with colorful flowers, ready to be picked. Barman took a deep breath. He wanted to be at peace with the mountain. He inhaled a gentle fragrance. This was the journey of an old man.

The sight of a house—red roof, white walls—emerged from behind the foliage. The whiteness of walls was blinding in the sunlight. *A house of light.* Squinting in the bright light, Barman closed his eyes briefly and then he decided to head for the house. There was a road in front of the house, but he had to search for a way to get there. Perhaps he would have to descend the hill and climb up the opposite slope. From the top of the hill where he was standing, he could see in all directions. Below, there was a bus stop, a market, and people the size of toys. He wiped his feet. *Hey, if you can't go on, then just say so.* No, he could do it; he was still strong, very strong. Going to that house would mean abandoning his plan. *Who lived there?* Barman suspected that the person who lived there was the stranger he saw that morning. Barman wanted very much to speak with that man; he wanted to spend some time with him.

He had already descended the hill. The gully was not too deep. He crossed the grass and waded through the overgrowth. The sun began to roast him as he ascended the last slope, lessening the mountain chill. Every inch of his skin was damp. His clothes were pasted to his skin. Under his hat, sweat saturated his white hair. There were beads of sweat on his brow and on the tip of his nose. Barman wiped the drops off against his arm. He didn't care! He was standing in front of the house. Vines with purple and red flowers wound up the trunk of a tree. The white wall that he had seen from the distance was the side of the house. *Who is inside?* There were dried leaves and dead flowers scattered about. *Hmm, this is not a house of light. It's the house of a lazy person!*

Barman wanted to rest. He could sleep anywhere, but it wasn't appropriate for him to sleep beneath the trees in front of the house. He knocked on the door, expecting someone to answer it. His legs were shaking; they were cramping and quite painful. The sweat on his skin chilled him. His sweaty hands were clammy and cold. *Your body's losing heat, Barman.* Ah, he had to go in, no matter what. There was no use for manners now. He could sleep on the chair inside. He peered through the glass window, which instantly clouded up with the steam from his breath. He wiped the glass as if to assure himself that nothing was wrong except that he was exhausted and wanted to sit down. *Why did he have to go inside? Only idiots sit on the ground outside when there are chairs inside.* He touched the doorknob. *Yes, good luck!* The door was unlocked. He immediately went inside. He dropped his hat and cane down and lay down on the sofa. In a short while, he was fast asleep.

A man as old as Barman stood on the terrace. He peered inside, wiping the glass pane on the door as if erasing the image of himself. It was clear. Someone was inside. He saw himself. No, the person inside was someone else; it was not him. The man was surprised: that person truly resembled himself. *If it is me, then why am I sleeping there?* He had not yet opened the door; he wiped his feet that were covered with dry grass on the floor. Just as his own things often were, the man's hat and cane were lying on the floor. As always, he took off his hat and threw it on to the table, then propped his cane up against the wall near the door. It was strange to look at this image of himself. *Is this a dream?* He slapped his thighs. *No. This is the real world.* Then he realized that he had just seen this person. The man's appearance that morning had completely surprised him. He had come upon the man early in the morning on the mountain and he had run away because their similarities had startled him. *Hmm, surely there were two people. That man and himself. But who was lying down? That man or himself?* Ah, he cursed himself. *Old scoundrel!* He laughed. He was confused because he was exhausted. "Sleep," he said to the old man inside.

He closed the partially open door so that the wind would not sneak in. "If you're sweating, it's not good to be exposed to the wind." He stood on the terrace for a long time, forgetting that he needed to rest as well. He searched for the best place to watch the guest from the outside. *Your face, brother, you're so thin! And your nose, it's sharp. Maybe that's because you don't have any more teeth, ha ha! Where are your teeth? Ah, it appears that they are still intact. Your muscles are just like wire, strung along with your skin.* Now, it was clear to him. Indeed, this man was indeed real.

He opened the door. A gust of wind blew into the house. He closed the door gently, afraid to awaken his guest. He observed his guest's face closely, as if searching for the smallest lines. *You're an old geezer.* He would prepare food for the guest. *Ah, if you wake up before I'm done, then we will celebrate this meeting. Ha ha!* He had several slices of bread that he had bought from the market. He got them out of the kitchen cupboard. *I'm not eating rice today, brother.* He placed the slices of bread on a plate. There was an open container of butter that he placed next to the plate on the guest's table. He brought a sheet of used paper out from the kitchen and placed it on the table, then he hurried back to the kitchen. He returned with a piece of charcoal in his hand. He wrote on the paper, "Forgive me, Sleepy One."

He thought about what he had done. He felt satisfied and stood up, smiling. Then he headed for the kitchen and removed his warm clothing. He was sleepy and tired. He had been walking since early morning. He was weary and now he wanted to sleep. He would be refreshed when he woke up. That was his work: wearing out his body and sleeping. The guest was still sleeping soundly. After eating, he went into his room and tried to lose himself in sleep.

When Barman woke up, he was very hungry. The first things he saw were the bread and butter. Poppy always prepared something for him on the table in his bedroom. He read the writing on the paper. He looked around the room, in all of the corners and at the furniture. This house was foreign to him. Everything, even the food. *Who was so good-hearted to provide food for someone who dared to enter his home?* This could happen only here on this mountain.

As he swallowed the last bites of the bread, he felt the pleasing warmth of the room. He saw his hat on the table and his cane, then he remembered his long walk. *Ah, Poppy is surely waiting for you, Barman.* He stood up and picked up his hat and cane. He hesitated. *A good person is someone who knows gratitude.* That thought spurred him to look further around the house. He found an old man asleep in the bedroom. His skin was wrinkled and thin! He was lying with his shirt open, baring his ribs. *I know this person. It's the man from this morning!* He was sleeping like an innocent child. His lips curved up slightly. *Surely this is the person who gave me the food.* Barman wanted to wake the man, but no, he wouldn't. He could still say thank you without the person hearing it, so he said: "Thank you. But your house is a mess." He saw papers, cans, and dust. He went into the other rooms. He looked around the kitchen. There were no books. Dirty clothes hung in the room, in the kitchen, on doorknobs. *What do you do so that you neglect your house like this? This cannot continue. At some time, you must be introduced to civilization.* He closed the door quietly and he left the house.

"Poppy, Poppy!"

He called from a distance. He didn't know when he had begun to miss Poppy, but he did. First he saw her image behind the door, then she emerged from the house. It seemed as if she had been waiting for him in the living room. Barman stumbled over the grass. Seeing Poppy coming out to meet him, he suddenly felt very old. But the bitter feeling passed quickly and he soon forgot about it.

"I took a long walk, Poppy. I saw everything there is to see here. Ravines, hills, trees!"

He spoke loudly, releasing the heaviness from his heart. But Poppy worried him.

"I'm so happy," she said.

But you make me sad, he thought.

"Oh, Papa! You must be exhausted," said Poppy.

The woman led Barman to the terrace. The man felt his weariness. His steps were heavy. Poppy's presence could not erase his exhaustion.

"Oh, your clothes! Come, put on some clean ones."

Poppy was busy with his clothes. She rushed into the bedroom and returned with a shirt. She looked at Barman again.

"And the pants as well!"

She went back into the room and returned with trousers in the evening light. She hesitated. She needed to help Barman get dressed.

"What did you do today?"

"Nothing. Just walked."

Barman massaged his feet.

"Sit down. You should take these clothes off and take a bath. Ah, you haven't had lunch yet either."

"Yes, I just realized that my pants are dirty!"

"You must have played in the dirt!"

"No. Never. I just walked."

"Yes. That's a kind of play, isn't it? Walking is a game for old men. Next time please be a bit more careful, okay?"

"Yes. I was playing!"

Barman almost shouted, *Aren't you my toy, too, Poppy?* "Come on, where're my clothes?" *You are always taking care of me, Poppy.*

"Just a moment. This must be cleaned first. Bathe with warm water. Get dressed and then eat. Are you very hungry?" *You can get your clothes dirty every day, Papa,* she thought.

"Not really."

Barman remembered the bread on the table that he had gobbled up. Poppy did everything for him. He liked to praise her diligence. *You are diligent, you are caring, you are pretty, my Poppy. You are here just for me all day long.* But poor Barman. *Have you ever seen an*

extraordinarily beautiful marble statue? That is your Poppy, old man.
Barman stopped suddenly in the middle of the meal he was eating
after his bath. He slid into misery. Poppy looked at him carefully.

"What's bothering you, Papa?"

That evening Barman stayed in his room. He wanted to
telephone Bobby to ask for a notebook. It would be useful to keep
a journal. But, no. He wanted to discard his memories. Once he
had written in a journal with big letters: "Forget yourself." Then he
threw the book away. He wanted to enjoy life. He wanted to say
farewell to everything that had passed. Thoughts swirled around in
his mind. Many questions as well. He tried to resist the onslaught
of thoughts and questions. He stood up and opened the cupboard
door. He closed it again. He opened and closed it repeatedly.
Poppy was busy in the back of the house. He wanted to hide in
the cupboard. Silently. No one would look for him; no one would
know him. There was a large cupboard in the corner of the room.
He stood up and opened the door. Some of Poppy's clothes were
hanging inside. He looked through the clothes and decided he
wanted to see his lover in these colorful dresses. He ran to the back
of the house. Poppy was washing her hands in the sink.

"Poppy," he said. "Look, this is what I want!"

He was excited about his new idea. He pulled Poppy by her
hand and led her to the room. Poppy followed calmly.

To her surprise, Barman said, "Some time you must wear this,
this, and this, okay?"

Poppy nodded, straightening her clothes in the cupboard. She
closed the door tightly. Barman was glad that he no longer wished
to hide in it. When Poppy returned to the back of the house,
Barman went to the living room and looked out at the fading
evening sky. He was delighted to watch bats flying among the
trees. He imagined that he could hear the flapping of their wings.

They sky outside darkened, but it was brightly lit inside the house. Poppy closed the curtains.

"It's nighttime, Papa," she said.

"Hmm," replied Barman.

Barman did not want to sleep that night. He gazed at the ceiling. Poppy tried to calm him. She reminded him that there were no problems on this mountain. There was nothing to be worried about. Not in the least. Barman was about to protest. *Perhaps there were not just a few problems, in fact there were many problems!* But he promised her he would close his eyes and go to sleep. Poppy watched Barman. His old forehead was furrowed.

"Papa, what should I cook tomorrow? What would you like? Or should I just open up some canned food again?"

Barman just looked down.

"What are you thinking about, Papa? Your worries are over. There's nothing to worry about anymore! Nothing! Even if we've finished all the food, we can just pick up the phone and ask Bobby to send something. Forget everything, except that we are alive!"

The last sentence made Barman look at Poppy for a long time. He turned towards her. She tried to unbutton his night shirt, but Barman said, "No, dear." Barman was afraid that the night would begin with disappointment. Poppy stroked his old head. *Go to sleep!* The old man rose and straightened the blanket that had slipped off Poppy. *I'm sorry, Poppy.* He didn't dare say it out loud, because he knew that the woman would reply as she had every night before that: It's all right, Papa. No, he did not want to suffer that disappointment every night.

When the sun touched the tip of the house, Poppy awoke to find only the crumpled blanket. Barman was not in the room. She was worried. Barman had never woken up this early. Still wearing her nightdress, Poppy searched through the house. Then she saw that the front door was unlocked. Barman must have gone out very early in the morning. The morning breeze wafted through the folds of her clothes as she circled the house. The sun was red in the east. Mist hung on the trees. Her sandals were wet from the dew on the grass. *Where are you, old Barman?* She was sure that the old man had left the house. *But where did you go, Papa?* The air was still damp and cold. She hurried back to the house. She would have to tell Bobby immediately. *I cannot take care of your father.* Is that what she would say to him? When the telephone operator asked her who she wished to speak to, she hesitated. *Perhaps Bobby didn't need to be told. The old man will have to return to the house eventually.* To her mind, she was responsible of tending to the old man's needs in the house. Whatever happened outside the house was not her business. She would be ready to serve him anything—tea or coffee or wine. She hung up the phone.

Poppy decided to stay in the house. As long as she did what she was supposed to do in the house, she would be doing enough. She did not need to plunge into everything everywhere. Everyone had things to do, and what she needed to do was to provide everything for the man with whom she came to the mountains. *I'm an ordinary woman, not a doctor. Whatever I do is enough.* She was prepared to take off her clothes and endure the cold and discomfort, stark naked. That was part of what she had to do; that was her job. She enjoyed the job and she decided to fulfill it, no matter what happened. She would not change her mind, because it had made her happy. When the old man came home, she would clean him up and welcome him back. She would be pleased to kiss his wrinkled cheek, stroke his white hair, and trace the lines of his old skin. She would dress without Barman having to praise her: "You are so beautiful in that dress, Poppy." She would dress to please him because it was her duty. And now, when Barman was gone, she would stay in the house peacefully and do her job. She would let the man do whatever he wanted, no matter what.

Barman knocked on the door to the house. The sun was red in the east, birds twittered in the trees. Several tiny gray birds nesting above the door flew about, pecking at the man's head. A young bat fell near his feet, flapping its wings. He looked about briefly and then knocked again. Harder.

"Are you deaf?" He cursed.

He moved to the window at the side of the house. He guessed that the resident of the house was sleeping near the window. He knocked loudly. He could not hear any sounds from within. He placed his ear against the window, hoping that he would hear loud snoring. He climbed up on the window ledge to search for a hole to peek through.

"Ha ha ha!" Someone laughed behind him. "What are you doing? Do you think that you're the only one who can wake up early?"

Barman stopped. He was balancing on the window ledge. *This is strange. He's already outside of the house so early in the morning.*

"What are you doing?" said the man again.

Yes, what are you doing? He didn't like questions. *He wasn't doing anything, actually. He knew that he was climbing up on the window ledge, but what for, he didn't really know. Hmph!* The moment passed. He was pleased, as if nothing had happened.

"What are you looking for, friend?" said the man.

Barman was silent. The question confused him. *Drat! The man was approaching him.*

"Wait!" the man said. "Come on, let's go in! I'll tell you what you're really looking for. Everyone who comes to this mountain is searching for something. I know that."

Barman peered at the man from his head to his foot. He was no longer in doubt; this was definitely the man who had given him the bread. This was the resident of this house. Barman had a strange feeling; his heart fluttered.

"I still have a bit more food, would you like some? Surely you haven't eaten yet. There's fresh fish, some game, some bread as well. We have not yet celebrated our meeting. Consider us to be old friends. At the very least, we have many things in common. I will teach you how to live!"

Like a tame buffalo, Barman quietly followed the man into the house. He was speechless. The man had caught him by surprise. They went to the dining table, which was neatly set. How different it was from the previous day! The floor was swept clean. Barman saw that the spider's web that was hanging in the corner yesterday was now gone.

"Your house is so clean!" Barman said in praise.

"Let us celebrate our meeting, my friend. I knew you would come here."

"Forgive me, I thought you were lazy."

"There are no lazy people on this mountain. Everything you see here is a product of my own handiwork. Nature very generously provides food for those who live here."

Barman looked at the food on the table. There were things there that he had never seen before. Was this the way the man spent his time on this mountain? His new friend was cheerful as he served him food. There was no sign of advanced age in him, except for his muscles. Barman guessed that the man still had a long life ahead of him. Time was on his side. Had he befriended time so that he would never age? *But time is our enemy*, thought Barman.

"Friend, come, help yourself!"

Barman thought about Poppy. Surely she had already prepared his breakfast. He knew that he should be happy with her, with the clean house and all the food that she prepared. She took care of everything. Everything. Everything.

"You're happy, aren't you?" he said and he started to eat.

Actually, Barman was not accustomed to the simplicity of the food, but it was invigorating. He did not know whether the meat was chicken or rabbit. But what was the point of asking? And the river fish. There were no clean flowered plates and napkins here or vegetable garnishes like the ones that Poppy always made. Also, the tomato was just left on the table. *This is very neatly done, for a man.* He found the food delicious prepared this way. He was actually even more impressed with his host than with the food that was served.

The old man invited Barman to spend more time there.

"Time," said the friend, "is something that we must savor. As with everything else."

Barman replied, "Yes, we must eat time or time will eat us!" And he laughed.

"We are friends. We must be friendly!" his host continued. "Why should we be enemies?"

They prepared for a journey for old men.

"This is a journey for grandfathers," said the friend.

There were fishing rods in the house. Barman was taken to the back of the house where there was a path.

"Do you want to fish with a rod or a net, my friend?"

"I'm not accustomed to river water," said Barman.

His friend just laughed. "You must learn from this life."

"Eh, do you think we should bring eggs?" he added. "And we shouldn't forget matches. You look like someone who had an unhappy childhood. Am I right? Now is the time to revisit your past. For an adventure in the mountains."

Barman was still studying his new friend. Unlike their previous encounter, now the man seemed to enjoy talking.

"Are we going far?"

"For the people of the mountain, it's close. But why should we care?"

The man pointed in a direction, his finger moving, drawing a circle in the air. They left the yard. When they reached the pine trees, Barman remembered something. He stopped.

"What?" asked his new friend.

"I forgot. I haven't asked you what your name is."

"My name is Humam. What's your name?"

"Barman."

"But, um… Why do we care? One name is as good as another. I actually don't have a name anymore. I'm just something like everything else. Here, names have no use."

Barman recalled again the days he had spent walking. He always walked without a name and without knowing the names of other people. What was the difference between the city and the mountains? Names were all lost amongst the trees.

"Humam, Hum or Mam? Can we get to a telephone?"

Barman remembered Poppy. He wanted to tell her about his trip.

"What for? We don't need anything else. We're already lost."

Barman didn't understand what Humam meant, but he honored it. He admired his new friend.

"And then?"

"Solitude is our essence."

"Your children? Your wife? Your family? Your friends?"

"I've let them all go."

"Everyone?"

"Yes."

"And me?"

"Our meeting is different, my friend. It's a mere coincidence. Our relationship is not a relationship."

They were silent for a while. Barman tried to understand his new friend: an old man who lived by himself. His thoughts wandered until Humam touched his hand.

"Be careful!"

They were walking on the edge of a ravine.

"If you're worried about me, then you shouldn't be, my friend. Because that is exactly what I do not do. There's nothing to worry about. Life is unfolding before us, and everything is well. I have released all of my burdens."

This man he'd just met raised more questions for Barman than he had answers. Barman thought, *this is a disaster*. He sighed, remembering Poppy at the house. Unconsciously, he hit his forehead with his hand. The man was satisfied with his solitary life, while Barman felt tormented in his life with Poppy.

When Barman turned to look at his friend, this man who had presented him with such a puzzle said, "My existence is my non-existence," and he added, as if he were talking to himself, "Or the opposite."

They had put their supplies into a backpack. Barman saw that his friend was tiring under its weight. He offered to take the pack, but Humam refused. Barman held the long fishing rod. He said that he wanted to be the model hiker with a pack on his back.

"Just carry this rod and your cane, my friend."

When the path started to go up an incline, Barman felt lucky that he was carrying only the cane and the fishing rod. The backpack would have weighed heavily on his shoulders. *But*, thought Barman, *our thoughts are far heavier than a backpack. They weigh down on our heads.* He was amazed. Humam was singing!

Throughout the entire journey towards the river, as they passed overgrown grass, gullies, and trees, Barman watched every movement his friend made. *Could a person survive like that?* He saw for himself how Humam's old eyes did not look tired during the uphill hike. It was true that his leg muscles were aged and swollen, but his face was fresh! As they walked, Humam gave him some advice.

"You are walking the wrong way, my friend. Enjoy this. We're walking together. Beneath you there is grass, water, earth, stones. Or you can run a race with your shadows. See the birds, feel the air, the fish, the river. There are clouds, clumps of earth, trees. Our new friendship is amazing! Our journey is our life!"

If this person had not been Humam, Barman would surely have already turned him away. How could anyone lecture Barman about a simple journey, whereas he, Barman, knew more about, for example, skiing? That would be absurd.

Humam continued, "Forget everything, even yourself. The only things here are the trees, the grass. You are the happiest of creatures. Time is to be enjoyed. Space is the place in which we move. Movement is our life."

"What do you mean?"

"I don't mean anything."

"I don't understand."

"Live in balance. Be as happy as you can be."

Barman tried to remember Humam's sentences in order.

"And death?" he asked.

"Death occurs when we do not move anymore."

"Aren't you afraid?"

"Death is actually the least terrifying event." Humam laughed unexpectedly and quickened his pace. "Ha ha! What were we talking about? Damn it!"

He started to run. Barman joined in the laughter and chased after him. It was soon clear that Humam was stronger than Barman. Humam stopped and waited for him.

"It's true, I'm stronger than you. But believe me... Your life will be a little bit longer than mine."

Barman regained his breath.

"But, 'Mam, Hum. Are you happy?"

"I don't believe in the existence of suffering."

"But what about hunger, fear, sickness, disappointment, loneliness?"

"I believe only in death. And that does not hurt."

They resumed their walk. The sun overhead threw shadows onto the grass below. They entered the pine forest. The trees were orderly. In the distance, they could hear the songs of the resin tappers. It was so shady and calm there. Barman prayed in his heart, quietly. He was afraid to speak. If he introduced another topic of conversation, Humam would bombard him with statements that he did not understand. The foliage of the trees completely protected them from the sun. They were alone with the towering trees, the voices of the tappers, the twittering of the birds, and the sound of the wind rustling through the trees. They followed a dirt path that wound around the trees in the middle of the forest. For a long time they walked without speaking. Birds perched in the treetops and chirped gaily. Occasionally, they would have to shuffle through piles of dry pine needles.

"I have a horse at home," said Barman, breaking the silence.

"I choose to live without a horse."

"It's nice."

"Mmm, I prefer to move my own muscles, because the essence of our life is motion. And even time will pass."

"A horse can bring enjoyment to life."

"My friend, you cannot add to or subtract from happiness. To be truly happy, you do not need anything other than yourself."

Who was this Humam? Was it true that he no longer had any family? That he did not know or was not known by anyone? Was he a hermit? No. Humam was just like any other person and just like

Barman himself. He didn't like suffering. Barman let the questions flow. *Was this the person who should be giving him advice? What, in fact, did he want from this man?* He had left his family, Bobby, Dosy, his grandchildren, and now he lived with Poppy who would always wait for him, as she was waiting for him today. He sighed unconsciously several times.

"What do you do, friend?" Humam asked.

"Actually, Hum, what are *you* doing on this mountain?"

"I'm not really doing anything. Life is over for me."

"Do you have any advice?"

"No."

"If there is any little thing, just tell me."

"Oh, yes. I think that I will not think any longer."

"You're not doing anything?"

"No. Everyone breathes. That's not *not* doing anything. You must be retired or rich, my friend. You've come to the mountain in search of a place to rest. That's what bothers you. Rest means that you want something. That's your mistake. I do not have any more wishes, any more wants. Not even rest."

They walked along a narrow path on the edge of a ditch flowing with clear water. The water splashed on to the sides of the ditch. Barman looked at the damp grass growing along the edges.

"This ditch flows to our river," Humam said. "Even our life flows somewhere. To the sea. To become rain and to flow in the river again."

A frog jumped up out of the water near Barman's foot. A drop of water splashed on to his trousers. He shook his leg to shake it off.

They stopped at a cliff. The walk had taken some time. The sun and the walk had dampened the backs of the two old hikers with sweat, soaking their shirts. A welcome breeze delighted them.

"There's the river," said Humam.

"It's so clear!"

The tops of large rocks rose out of the water. The river shimmered, reflecting the sun. From the top of the cliff, Barman could hear the gurgling of the water below. Parts of the river were flowing fast and there were parts where the water was calm. Nature revealed itself to Barman. The sun and clouds met with the green mountainside. Soft thin clouds lined the top of the mountain. The slopes were overgrown with wild grass and the trees were full of birds.

"It's a long walk," said Barman

"The problem is that you are counting time."

"There is someone waiting at home."

Barman thought of Poppy who was probably sitting, waiting for him in the living room. Her clear eyes—ah, like the river water—perhaps she was gazing off in this direction, hoping that Barman would emerge from behind the trees. *Poor Poppy, Poppyyyyy!*

"If that is how you live, then you will not be able to enjoy anything in life."

"But we must honor love."

"But even the clock will stop ticking."

Barman did not understand the old fisherman. He was silent. *It's no use to speak much with this man. Where did he come from?*

"If you are still counting, even time can kill you."

"But—!"

"What?"

"Lots of things, 'Mam, Humam."

"What we must think carefully about is where are we going to fish. Think carefully. Will the boulder we sit on be comfortable? Will the sun be too strong on our backs? That is what we should think about. Nothing else."

Humam scanned the entire river area. From the top of the cliff, the river sparkled. A shimmering light flowing through the greenery.

Finally, Humam said, "Friend, we'll go down over here. Be careful!"

Humam started down the slope. Barman very carefully followed his old friend. *Be careful, Barman. If you fall down there, someone will cry for you.* There was a bit of grass on the slope, the earth had hardened and stones in the path helped to ease their descent.

As they made their way down the hillside, Humam chattered. "Yes, concentrate on how to go down this slope. Which rocks are embedded deeply enough and which ones are not strong enough to support your footing? Look at the tree roots. See the trees on the cliff over there. Look at the water down there. And the sun overhead. Don't we feel recharged?"

They sat on a boulder beneath a tree whose branches stretched out over the river. They could reach the grass at the edge of the river in just one step. Humam decided to sit on the boulder.

He said, "Sit here. You'll feel like you are in the middle of the water, surrounded by water."

Humam quickly unpacked the fishing rod. He attached the bait and floater. Then he left the rod alone. The floater would signal if the bait had been taken. Barman recalled images of philosophers and Chinese poets fishing. *Was Humam a poet or a philosopher?* Although his face was wrinkled and old, Humam's eyes glowed the joyful light of someone who had achieved something in his life. Meanwhile Barman felt as if he had lost something, that he was searching for something and had not yet found it. And some kind of anxiety was constantly haunting him. Barman looked at his new friend with jealousy and curiosity. *How could a person's eyes shine like that? Humam's eyes were like those of a child! Would he find wisdom through fishing? Oh, he would crush those thoughts! We're children!* Suddenly, Barman took off his shoes. He never went barefoot. His naked feet had white soles. They were thin. He threw his shoes onto the grass under the tree at the river's edge. Then he dipped his feet into the water. When he pulled them out, they were cool. When he dipped them in for the second time, the water felt refreshing, not cold. The coolness of the water seeped into his body. He laughed at himself. They were two old men playing in the river. He felt rejuvenated.

Here, in the river water, under the trees, shaded by nature and surrounded by rocks, he felt very far from the people he loved, but he also felt something new, something that made him happy. He glanced at Humam and smiled. He felt free. There was no one who would chastise him if he ate, slept, or pooped wherever he wanted to. He realized that it was only here that a person could have complete power over himself. He began to feel comfortable. He put his feet back in the water. He observed them carefully; the skin was wrinkled. He began to feel drowsy. He jumped over to the bank of the river under the trees. He spread his jacket on the grass and lay down on it. As the wind blew through the trees above, Barman was carried off to sleep.

Humam glanced at his new friend. Barman was fast asleep. Humam smiled. He was a clever fisherman. He had caught several fish. He wanted to do something to surprise his sleeping friend, so he hoped that Barman would not wake up too soon. He worked very carefully. He restrained himself from shouting or saying anything when he lifted the fish from the water. He planned to cook it and serve it for their lunch. He wanted to celebrate this meeting with his new friend in nature. Every child who returns to his father must be praised. This was a very good idea, and he was happy to be holding the fishing rod. He was excited about surprising Barman when he woke up. Humam did not want to awaken his friend to ask for his help because he wanted to surprise him. He knew that there were dry branches around for a fire. He cleaned the fish, seasoned it with spices he had brought, wrapped it in leaves, and roasted it. He imagined how amazed his friend would be with his cooking. Humam hummed.

Humam did everything by himself. When Barman woke up, Humam would smile at him and begin to talk while the sleepy man was still only half awake.

"Nature is the Divine One. We are only a small part of It. Do not be sad or happy. Return to Nature. Nature will welcome you. As you have welcomed your own life."

Then Humam would really wake up his friend. He would pull the hairs on Barman's leg. And when Barman rubbed his eyes to get reacquainted with his surroundings, Humam would shout: "This is your second birthday! In true freedom! As perfect as perfect can be! Like the mountain air, like the water that flows from the mountain spring, like the birds in the sky!"

He would shout out loud, resolutely. Yes, that is what he would do.

3

The experience with Humam had amazed Barman. The old man had taught him many things. Barman was weary when he returned home that evening. He had lost interest in all the heroes in his books; in fact, he hated them. Now he had to admit that it was Humam, more than anyone else, who impressed him.

Poppy welcomed him home.

"I've been waiting for you all day, Papa. Every sound near the door made me think about you. I thought to myself, maybe that's Papa. Even the twittering of the birds sounded like your footsteps. Why were you out so long?"

Barman was pleased with this greeting, but he was exhausted. He turned down Poppy's offer of a meal. This was the first time that he had declined to eat. Poppy suspected that he must have eaten somewhere else. He told her that he preferred to lie down and he asked her to massage his feet. Poppy led him to the bedroom where she helped him to change his clothes. While Poppy massaged his feet, Barman recalled what Humam had said about women: "Let go of all of your possessions. Whatever you own, in actuality, owns you, and you will never be free. You think you have power, but you don't. Your possessions strangle you; they tie you down!"

As Barman recalled those words, he looked at Poppy. *Who is the master now and who is the servant?* Poppy's soft hands lightly touched his rough skin; her gentleness seeped deeply into his soul. Suddenly, he wept.

"Why are you crying, Papa? Does it hurt?"

"No, it's nothing, Poppy. It's just that I realize how much I love you at this moment."

"I already know that, Papa."

"No, you don't know how much."

He could not restrain his feelings. Poppy had suffered because of him. Barman could not agree with Humam if he meant that it was this woman who made him suffer. It was just the opposite.

"Why are you doing all of this for me, Poppy?"

Poppy was silent. She stopped massaging him. She leaned over to Barman's ear.

"I want to serve you, Papa," she said firmly.

Once more, Barman looked into Poppy's eyes. He searched for reassurance in those eyes. He believed her, but he was perplexed. *Why did she choose to do this?* Exhaustion soon carried him off to a restful sleep. But soon, he cried out again for his Poppy. She had given him everything, but Humam had said that her devotion was "strangling" him.

Would he ever free himself from Poppy? That morning had been his first experiment in freedom, but in the end he had returned to her. In any case, if Bobby knew about his behavior, he would not condone it, especially if Barman tried to send Poppy away. If Barman ever succeeded in distancing himself from Poppy, who would be the one to leave the house—Poppy or him? Humam had invited Barman to live with him at his house. Ah, how stupid that old man was! They would become close friends and that would be a bond. A bond that was not a bond, Humam had said at the time.

Barman got up from his nap. The sun had set and he felt dizzy. He called to Poppy; she was sitting nearby, waiting for him. He asked her to rub his forehead with some aromatic oil, so Poppy brought him lemongrass oil, which warmed his forehead. In a few moments, the warmth dispersed the dizziness. He decided that he wanted to do something for her.

"Would you like me to take you shopping at the market, Poppy?"

Poppy knew that Barman wanted to do something for her, so even though she didn't need anything, she acceded to his wishes. She nodded. She still had vegetables, preserved foods, dried meat, and canned goods. She could just telephone Dosy in the city and the driver would come, bringing everything they needed. If Barman had not suggested it, she would not want to walk all the way to the market near the city bus stop.

Instead, she replied, "Papa, there are fresh vegetables at the market! Everything is still fresh. Imagine, every day it's just like that."

The next morning, Poppy prepared the shopping basket. Barman reached for it.

"This is my job, Poppy. A woman shouldn't carry the basket."

Since Barman carried the basket, Poppy let her arms swing freely. As they walked, Barman glanced at Poppy from time to time and assured himself: *She's mine. It's not the other way around. This is Poppy, a beautiful woman.* He had known many beautiful women in his life and Poppy was prettier than all of them. He should be happy. He wanted to forget everything Humam had said. *No, I am not her possession; rather, she is my possession. She's mine. Who would be willing to let go of a woman as beautiful as her?* Even though he might suffer, he could not let her go. *Poppy, Poppy.* He admitted that he would not be able to own his Poppy entirely. He always failed at night. That disappointed him, but Poppy always said that it didn't matter. *It doesn't matter, Papa.* She said that to set him at ease. *Or did she mean that he could not have complete power over her?* These feelings, like his weary thoughts, tumbled about in his mind. *Poppy had tied him down to a schedule: a time to eat, a time to sleep, what clothes to wear. Come home. Could he give all of that up as Humam had done?* In the past, he had felt that something was missing in his life and he had come to this mountain to search for it. But now he felt that either he had too much and he couldn't handle it all, or that he had too little so that life was difficult. The image of Humam emerged in front of him. He stopped.

"What is it, Papa?"

"It's nothing, my dear."

He resumed the walk, trying to hide his thoughts from Poppy.

The market was located at some distance from their house. In the front of the market there was a stop for the buses and mini-vans that traveled back and forth from the market to the city. Poppy led Barman into the market. She bought vegetables, meat, and fruit. She also asked Barman what he wanted her to cook. The basket filled up, as if they'd bought everything in sight. Barman looked around at the bustle of the marketplace and he felt lonely. The people there did not appear to pay any attention to him. They were going about their own businesses, trading their merchandise. Were these the machines of the marketplace?

Barman insisted that he wanted to carry the basket, but Poppy refused.

"We should look for a porter, Papa."

Barman thought she meant: you are too old for this, too old to carry a shopping basket. *Hmph!* Barman asked her if he should look for a porter, and Poppy agreed.

Poppy waited and waited for Barman and the porter. *Good gracious! That old man had been gone for an hour.* Poppy was afraid that something may have happened and she steeled herself for any surprises. She wanted to stay calm, no matter what happened. She searched for a porter to carry her basket and then she began to walk home with him.

Poppy looked back into the market for one last search just in case Barman appeared, but there was no sign of him. Standing on a grassy slope, near a row of sparsely spaced houses, she decided not to tell Bobby anything about this, even though he often asked for news. She knew that Barman would return.

When she reached the house, Poppy told the porter to put everything in the kitchen. She felt as if there was something missing in the house. *Yes,* she thought, *of course, old Barman had not returned home with her.* All she had to do was prepare a meal for him. When Barman arrived home, the meal would be ready. What more could she do? She had to play out the role that she had chosen on the mountain. While Barman was gone, there was no one around who would object to her singing or to any other expression of her happiness. She was busy throughout the day; the time passed quickly.

When Poppy went to throw out the kitchen trash that evening, Barman was standing in the garden in the midst of the flowers. He had returned, just as she had guessed he would. The bird returned to its nest! This had happened before. Yes, the man had crawled through the flowers once before. She smiled at Barman. She put down the basket of trash and approached the flowers, inhaling their fragrance. A leaf from the rose bush fell at her feet. She was at the edge of the flowerbed.

"Papa?"

"I'm home, Poppy."

Barman's voice was weak and soft, slipping into exhaustion. The previous evening, she remembered well, Barman had played with her in the garden. Now, more than ever, she saw the old man as he really was. Forgetful, hunched, listless. His head was buried under his hat, hiding his white hair. His clothes were wrinkled. *Ah, something has happened to you, Papa.* Poppy smiled. Barman stiffened with her greeting. The old man was bewildered. Poppy seemed to have been waiting for him. If he wasn't Barman, she would be greeting a stranger. Poppy welcomed him.

"Why have you come out to greet me?" Barman asked.

"I was expecting you, Papa. I like you like this. It pleases me."

The conversation was awkward.

"Do I still have to go in the house?"

Poppy laughed at the question, then she stopped suddenly. Surely there was something behind that odd question. She laughed again: no, nothing had happened. Poppy wanted to get past the awkwardness quickly. She stepped into the flowerbed and pulled Barman out.

"I already said that I would always wait for you, no matter what happens. Remember that, Papa. Everything is prepared for you. I like serving you. Don't ever worry again, Papa. It's my decision to be here. I'm content with everything here."

Poppy looked at the old man. She wanted to say something else.

"I think, Papa…" She stopped to watch Barman.

"Say it, Poppy."

"Your one fault is… hmm…"

"Say it!"

"You think too much."

Barman wiped his forehead. The flowers in the trees swayed on their branches.

"Don't think any more, Papa. Just live! Aren't all your problems already over?"

"It appears that my life has just begun."

"Yes, it has. After dinner, you must have a good long sleep."

The fading sunlight on the tops of the trees announced that night was approaching. The birds soared, touching the leaves, gently flapping their wings. The mountain was quiet. Poppy guided Barman to the house. The man let himself be led. The coffee that she prepared for him warmed his body. He wanted to beg for the woman's forgiveness.

"All of a sudden, Poppy, I wanted to leave you. Forgive me."

"I know. You won't leave anyone again."

"I'm ashamed."

Poppy left him sitting in the front room as she prepared dinner.

She shouted from the kitchen, "You must be very hungry, aren't you?"

He could hear the sound of plates in the kitchen.

Poppy wanted Barman to stay in the house. She told herself that the old man was important to her. She hoped that the presence of the man and his age, which would test her patience, would provide her something she needed: purity, peace. This is what she wanted.

That evening when she brought wine to Barman, she said, "You don't have to go anywhere, Papa. I want you to stay here all the time."

Barman sighed a long sigh. The wine warmed his body. He was very sleepy. He could think of nothing but sleep. He was exhausted from walking and thinking. Poppy said, "Sleep, Papa. When you wake up tomorrow morning, you'll be refreshed!"

He didn't know why, but that thought pleased him. It was starting to get cold outside. He asked Poppy to stay near him. He said that there was nothing more pleasing than the chill of the mountain and the warmth of a woman's touch. He hoped that in this way he would please her, but when Poppy came to him, he felt wistful. He remembered Bobby, he remembered Humam. What were they doing on a night like this? The day's journey and the bustle of the market had made him feel lonely. He recalled the shouts of the children in the market, the vendors, the buses, and the sweaty porters. He saw himself now on the mountain, lying in bed with Poppy. He pulled up Poppy's blanket that had slipped off.

He thought about his solitary life. The mountain around him was silent and cold. The universe seemed to leave him alone. He imagined a bird sleeping in the tree, huddled in the warmth of its feathers, withstanding the cold. Water crystals frozen on the branches, leaves slowly drifting down, pine trees standing quietly, challenging the heavy black sky. The residents of the mountain homes, the deserted marketplace, dogs howling in the darkness.

He sensed that the world was full of secrets; it was astounding. How magical the nights were! Here he was: in the center. Alone. Not understanding anything. Tomorrow morning he would wake up. There was nothing he needed to do. His thoughts returned to the old cities and secrets of his dim past. Bobby lived down there amongst the lights in the distance that he could see from the mountain. He wanted to weep. He no longer lived in the city. His future was here! But even here, there was nothing for him to do. He was just a meaningless object on the mountain, submerged in the secret of nature, the dark nights. He was unknown and unknowing. The world and life went on as he watched helplessly. *Bobby, Dosy, Poppy, the old fisherman, where are all of you at a moment like this?* Gradually, his eyes pressed him into a deep sleep.

Early in the morning, Poppy woke up. She looked at Barman closely.

"Papa, your eyes are swollen. You didn't sleep very much last night!"

Barman gazed emptily at her as she tidied up the bed. Barman wanted to hide his face. He was afraid that his face would reveal more about his restlessness than his mouth would.

"There are stains on the pillow! Were you crying last night? Why? What happened?"

There was no one who knew why, even he himself did not know. *Be quiet, Poppy, Poppyyyy.*

Poppy stopped questioning him. Barman was pleased that Poppy understood that the tears on the pillow must have been shed when he was asleep. She knew that she often found her own tearstains on her own pillow. But she was stronger than the old man. She smiled to see the tearstains. Perhaps it was not a sign of sadness, but a sign that he was pleased, overjoyed.

She was living a life that she had deliberately chosen. She had willingly made this decision; she was truly happy to accept this situation. When Bobby offered her the job as his father's companion, she had agreed immediately. Thank you, she said to him. Bobby was amazed that she didn't ask for anything. *Bobby, it's my own business, don't mess it up.* In truth, she was happy here on the mountain. She had never thought about the kind of happiness that she was experiencing now. *Will this be over soon or will it last forever?* She didn't want to think about that. She wanted to stop thinking. This new life was her freedom.

She had to go on this journey to the mountain. She would take this time to cleanse herself. She constantly reminded herself to smile graciously when she saw how the old man was weak, nervous, and wrinkled. He was vastly different from the men who always came to her when she was in the city. She would become a different person. No, she would not admit that she was voluntarily undergoing punishment. She would not say anything now; she would no longer judge her life. *Live, Poppy, live.* That is what she whispered to herself whenever she forgot and started to think about her life.

Poppy had asked Bobby if his father would be angry if he ever found out about her past life. Bobby had said that his father treated everyone equally and that he would be happy with a beautiful woman at his side. "My father is not a holy man, Poppy," Bobby had said. "You'll be a good couple," he added. Poppy had never thought whether anyone would be a good match for her. She let Bobby think whatever he wanted. She constantly reminded herself: *If you have stopped thinking about yourself, then don't expect other people to think about you.*

Poppy was happy on the mountain. No one paid for her services and she didn't have to surrender herself to anyone, except when Barman asked for her. *That old Barman!* The man wanted to savor everything he could with her, even though Bobby once said that his father only asked for Poppy to take care of him, nothing more. It was not her fault that Barman did not get anything from her body. She had already offered herself to him. Bobby had told her that Barman liked to roam around the city to forget his frustrations with women. In truth, the man did not have to be fussed over; he was just too old. Complete rest on a distant mountain was far better than dreaming of a youthful life that would only lead to disappointment. Had Bobby exiled his father? Was he willing to spend money for that?

In the morning Barman was sitting in the living room. Poppy approached him to comb his white hair.

"Papa, what's happened?"

"There is no place for me, Poppy, no place anywhere."

Barman evaded Poppy's touch and mumbled his response again. Poppy let him open the front door. The cool morning breeze touched her skin.

Poppy straightened up the bedroom, examining Barman's damp pillow again. *Poor old man!* She must be the cause of at least some of his sadness. But she could not let Barman leave her. She needed him. No matter what worried Barman, he had to remain by her side. She did not know what she would do if he was not with her. She did not dare to anticipate the future. She would move only if other elements in the world moved. She would build her life around someone else's life.

And now that someone else was Barman. She was willing to live with Barman in this new life, even if it went on forever. She wanted something different from her past. She constantly reminded herself that her life now was not one of voluntary suffering and striving to satisfy her desires. No, this was the only way to release herself from her past. She had been bored with her life. But now her passions were reviving; this was precious. *As for Barman, ah, everyone had their own concerns.* She would surrender everything that she had to the old man. And when it was over, she hoped that life would go on its own way. *Every element will perform its own role, and the world will go on, Poppy.*

The old man was her way to freedom, but not because she believed that selling her body to a man was a sin. She was disgusted with that. So, even though she always had to listen to Barman's disappointed complaint—"Poppy, there are no rights for the elderly"—she would console herself and the old man by saying: "That's all right, Papa." She could bear this kind of life. She could see the value of continuing like this. She found comfort in the fact that the mountain was cold and quiet, and that there was no one here who knew her. She could feel the difference compared to her life in the city where she was kept busy with so many clients who dragged her into a life of sin. Here, on the mountain, she would accept the old man with all the consequences. Even if he struck her, she would smile—a smile that would embody passion for a reviving life. The old man's problems were his thoughts. Thinking was dangerous for both of them. She realized now that life at this moment was not built on a foundation of thoughts. She decided that thoughts, memories, and dreams had been the cause of her suffering all this time; they had made her weary. Now the time had come to free herself. That is what she was doing here. Barman complained constantly because he did not want to accept the life he was supposed to live. That old man had an aptitude for suffering: desires, thoughts, memories, dreams.

"Papa, will you listen to me?" she said to Barman as she followed the old man wandering around the house.

She reminded Barman about the view. "The flowers are so beautiful. Isn't this a scorpion orchid, Papa?" and "What do you want to eat for lunch today?"

She peppered him with questions, fishing for a response. At Poppy's request, they sat under a pine tree. Long dry pine needles were scattered in the grass. Poppy slipped a blade of grass into her mouth and chewed on it as if she was just passing a leisurely morning. Once, in the distant past when she was still a young girl, she had spent a morning like this with someone else.

"What are you really thinking about, Papa?"

She was hesitant to ask the question, but it was better that she ask Barman to reveal his thoughts to her than to leave. There were many ways to forget about the past.

"Do you really want to know?"

"Why not?"

"There are so many thoughts. They're continuously invading my mind."

Barman pointed to something in the distance. A row of clouds moved towards the mountain peak. His eyes followed the clouds. Reflected in Poppy's dark eyes, the clouds moved as if they were in a magic mirror. Barman turned to look at the woman at his side.

"You must be suffering because of me, Poppy."

"I've never felt that way, Papa."

"You just don't want to realize it, perhaps."

"Why are you so depressed?"

Poppy was afraid to push the question further. She did not want to become involved in a problem that wasn't her concern, even though it was Barman's problem. She knew many men who poured their personal anxieties into sex. She had often been on the receiving end of their tantrums even though she never wanted to become entangled in their affairs. The men who came to her, at night or during the day, were worried about all kinds of things. They were throwing themselves away. For a long time, she had just accepted her fate. They were asking for her to surrender her body to them. As with the birds that twittered or sang, it made no difference to her whether it was a song of grief or joy. Every bird's call was a song. She had to convince Barman to stay at home.

"My thoughts are old men's thoughts, Poppy. Surely you don't want to hear them. I'm free from work, retired. It's very pleasant. Ever since I was young, I looked forward to this part of my life. I should be happy, but I'm not. Something is constantly bothering me, but I don't know what it is."

"What more do you want from this life, Papa?"

"Nothing." He stopped. "… Or something else."

"You're retired. What else is there?"

"If life is over, then we should put everything in order. But life is never over. It's as if eternity is right in front of me. Time— now it's time that imprisons me. I don't want anything in life, but time is making me think. Or perhaps I want something that is impossible."

Poppy laughed, then she stopped. She thought the sentiment was extreme.

"You don't understand what I mean, Poppy."

"I know, Papa. The answer is so easy!"

"What do you mean?"

"You think that this life is meaningless. That's ridiculous. Remember, you're still alive. You see the sun every morning. Every morning, just say that to yourself."

"I want to free myself, Poppy."

"What?"

"Free myself from time that is torturing me! From life! And its burdens!"

"That's suicide!"

"No, it's not that."

"That's not possible. Look at those birds flying there."

A flock of birds flew past them. They came perhaps from the distant rice fields.

"They live and they're happy. Fly, fly! For them, time is life itself. Always, always flying. What do they care?"

Then Poppy spoke about her decision to live on the mountain with Barman. It had taken courage, and it made her happy. Every moment of life was to be enjoyed. Time that flowed continuously was the biggest source of happiness for those who could savor it. Why did Barman think about the tortures of time? Poppy said that the passing of time was exactly the same whether a person felt they were being tortured or not. Time just went on.

"You're clever, Poppy."

"Life has taught me a lot, Papa, more than my days at university."

"You went to university?"

"Yes, two years."

"What did you study?"

"Philosophy."

"You're strange, Poppy. How... hmm. How did you come to this?"

"How indeed? Everyone becomes something. There are no exceptions."

Barman respected the woman. She was not the simple, stupid woman he had thought she was. No, Poppy deserved his admiration.

"Speak, Poppy."

"About what?"

"About your strange life!"

"There's nothing strange about my life. Or perhaps everything is strange. Everything can be understood or nothing can be understood. That's the problem. And I have decided to stop thinking. There's nothing to tell you about, Papa. Do you feel that it is necessary to search for the tracks of the rice field birds that just flew by? No. It's useless. So just live! Live!"

"That's not the civilized way."

"It's up to you. It's a kind of civilization, as long as the person living it is conscious of it!"

Barman stirred and stood up. He looked at Poppy sharply. He was impressed. Poppy smiled, as if saying that there was no longer anything that he needed to worry about. *Yes, it's me, Papa.* Poppy threw away the blade of grass in her mouth. For just a moment, Barman noticed how full her lips were, but then he immediately dismissed the thought.

"Yes, that's what I believe, Papa. Hmm, perhaps it's my religion."

The old man was still standing, stunned. This was a blow for him. He mumbled to himself. How that woman could live!

Suddenly Barman ran off. Poppy laughed and chased him. The sun beamed down on the two people chasing each other. The spirit of the old man and the young woman! They ran through the overgrown grass in back of the house.

Barman shouted from a distance, "It's a miracle!"

Poppy just laughed and chased him. They stopped and faced each other in the overgrowth. Barman was panting.

He said, "You don't like civilization."

Poppy tried to chase him through the grass.

Barman turned and said, "Poppy, you're just a beautiful bird."

Poppy laughed and circled around to chase him again. Finally Barman stopped; he had run out of breath. Poppy held his arm.

"It appears that women are stronger than men!"

Barman exhaled heavily. Beads of sweat dropped from his forehead. Poppy wiped them off with her hand, dampening her palm and her graceful fingers.

"Poor old man, Poppy."

"Poor lucky man, Papa!"

"Suffering!"

"Happy!"

"Tortured!"

"Cheerful!"

"The people in the market carry burdens on their backs, but I carry my burden here," he pointed to his head. "I saw myself and that burden when I was looking for a porter to carry our purchases. That's why I went off, Poppy. Can we just hand over our burdens to someone else?"

"Enough, Papa."

"Those people in the market, they have released their burdens."

"So have we!"

"Surely they must be happy. Some time I will meet with them."

"That won't be necessary, Papa."

They were both silent. Barman's breath started to return to normal. He said firmly, "Perhaps they're like you, Poppy. Happy, but without any position in society. I don't want that! That's contradictory!"

"What do you mean 'position'?"

"Life that has value."

"Life itself is a value," said Poppy. "You don't need anything else! If you're alive, you have meaning. If you're dead, you don't!"

"I object!"

"Anything more than that from life is useless! It's just empty words."

Poppy went on at length. She said that anything that did not have value was in opposition to life. Illness, for example. She said that it was more for health reasons than moral ones that she left the brothel. She didn't believe in morals. Everything that caused suffering, illness, and death must be seen as evil or just a worthless daydream. Whatever contributed to life had value. Poppy spoke with passion; Barman listened in amazement. It seemed as if Poppy was trying desperately to reassure herself.

The conversation with Poppy disturbed Barman. *It's a different perspective*, he thought. The woman posed new questions. *Could people live like that? No, he did not want to accept that point of view.*

Everyone should live their lives consciously; they should search for something of value. It was a moment of realization for him and he would share it with anyone who was willing to listen: it is time for us to reflect upon our lives.

When he got back to the house after this conversation, Barman wanted to telephone Bobby. He wanted to ask Bobby why he had chosen Poppy to be his companion. But his son would say that Barman himself had chosen her and then he wouldn't be able to say anything else. Or he would ask Bobby to replace Poppy with someone else.

He would not make that telephone call. It would just add to his son's burdens. *Poppy, Poppyyy,* he sighed. He wanted to hear his son's voice. He wanted to forget about his Poppy. He held the telephone receiver hesitantly in his hand. Then he rang his son.

"What's happened, Dad?"

"Ah, Bob. Can you send the horse?"

Actually, he was only grasping for something to say. Poppy heard him and said, "A horse? It will make a mess in the yard, Papa."

"A yard as big as this will not be messed up by only one horse, Poppy. The horse will find its own food."

There were two horses at Bobby's house. Both the father and the son liked horses. But it had been difficult to enjoy this hobby in the city. Ever since he began taking solitary walks in the city, Barman had forgotten about his horse. Bobby agreed to Barman's request and said he would send his father's favorite horse. Barman was thrilled.

His telephone conversation with his son had been good. With the horse he could challenge time. But then he realized that with a fast horse like that, everything else would seem slow. That would create another kind of suffering. He didn't know what to do.

Bobby sent the horse, along with a drawing for a stable and the carpenters to build it. At Barman's request, a stall was built on the side of the house. The workers were busy the entire day building it. In the evening, Barman looked at the stable and the white horse inside it. Several small gray birds twittered on the roof of the stable. Barman was not lazy. He shoveled the horse dung in the stable and deposited it in a pit at the edge of the yard. Poppy laughed at clumsy Barman. He replied that cleaning the stable was a proper job for a man and he forbade Poppy not just from helping him, but even from seeing the dung. *You shouldn't get your hands dirty, Poppy.*

Barman planned to ride his horse to search for new friends. *To hell with Humam!* He was going to forget that man. He wanted a fresh life. In fact, he promised Poppy, if she needed something from the market, he would ride the horse there with her shopping list. In short, he would help Poppy in whatever way he could. *Doing the housework together was important too, wasn't it?* He smiled, relishing the thought that at his advanced age, he was living with a young woman. It was a strange household! The woman provided everything for the man, but the man could not provide anything for her. Let the horse take him to distant places! If he ever got tired of the horse or if the horse got tired of him, he would tell Bobby to have someone take it away. The horse, as white as milk, seemed spotless in the morning light.

One morning Barman was busy with the horse in the stable. As long as he was occupied with the horse he forgot about his uneasiness on the mountain. He whistled contentedly. The stall was always clean. Poppy teased him and said that he was surely still a good rider. All of a sudden, Humam was standing at the stable door.

Pointing at the horse, Humam said, "We are that horse, my friend."

Barman turned to look at him. *Ah, it was that old man again.*

Humam smiled at him and continued, "Confined in the world. Without freedom or hope. Or with hope that is always only hope and nothing more. This world is our stable. Our prison! Except…" he held his breath. His eyes remained on Barman.

Barman stopped working. He leaned against the wooden wall of the stable. The shovel was in his hand. He slowly began to worry that the visitor was going to be a problem. *Leave, Humam! No, wait! Don't leave! I need you! I do!* The horse swished its tail. It pulled at the green grass.

"The horse is hungry," said Barman, changing the topic of conversation.

Barman opened the stable door and led the horse out. He wanted to show Humam that he did not want to think about anything else.

"This is the one and only thing that I like, Humam."

He patted the horse's back.

"This is a real riding horse."

He jumped onto its back like a bird hopping deftly onto a branch. He felt weightless. The horse pranced. Humam just stood, leaning against his cane, speechless.

"Look, Humam. I'm in love with this horse. We love each other. I cannot let it go."

Humam shouted from the distance, "Love is a link in the chains that restrain us!"

Barman was startled briefly, as if the horse was caught off guard. Then the horse began to prance again. Barman did not want to listen to anything.

From the distance, Humam continued to shout, "Love restrains us!"

Barman trotted the horse back and forth while Humam shouted those words.

From atop the horse, Barman replied, "I don't care, I don't care!"

Their voices competed with each other, getting louder and
louder.

Then Humam stopped shouting. The sun felt warm on his
back. He turned around and left the horse and rider behind.
Barman watched him go. He disappeared quickly behind a slope
and Barman could no longer see him. The old man stopped his
horse. For a long time he gazed in the direction that Humam had
gone. The horse began to pull at the grass at his feet. *Ah, that man!*
Barman could still see branches moving in the distance. *That must
be Humam.*

Sitting there on his horse, Barman became uneasy. He realized
that he could not stop caring about Humam. He had learned
something from that man during their first meeting. How could he
just erase Humam from his thoughts? Humam's words, unexpected
and thoughtful, always perplexed him. That man was like a wise
hermit. *Who was he an incarnation of—Muhammad, Jesus, or
Abiyasa?*

He could see Humam's house from his position on the top
of the horse. The horse was restless. His own house was quiet.
Perhaps Poppy was working in the kitchen. He wanted to show
her his riding skills. *He was always with that woman, night and day!*
Whenever he thought about her, his heart would pound, but then
he would become incredibly sad. *A faithful lover!*

He once noticed an empty look in her eyes that reminded him
of the apathetic faces of the people in the city. She could sleep
soundly even though he had difficulty closing his eyes at night.
He became suspicious of the woman, even though words of love
flowed from her lips every morning and evening. *Cheerfulness was
a machine named woman!* He felt nauseous. Indeed, he had once
accused her of being uncivilized. Apparently she didn't hear the
accusation. She always sang in the bathroom, in the kitchen, when
she was cooking, when she was mopping the floor, everywhere; she

was always singing! Life was over for her. Bobby had praised her for her quick and efficient service. He thought that it would be good for his father if there was a woman at his side. *You were wrong, my son. Look, I am actually suffering because of her. I don't know whose fault it is—hers or mine.*

Barman felt worthless. He tried to rid himself of that feeling by making his horse walk slowly around the garden. *Poppy was still very young.* He remembered the days of his youth: the Eiffel Tower, beaches brimming with joy, blond women who slept with him. The horse circled around the house. There were blades of grass and a bit of froth on its mouth. It was panting slowly. Barman exhaled a long sigh that poured forth from the depths of his heart.

Poppy called to him from inside the house, "Papa, Papa!"

Her clear voice blended with the morning breeze in the pine trees. Barman mused over her call. It was heartbreaking! He looked sadly in the direction of her voice. *Be silent, Poppy! I cannot hear you. I will not hear you, Poppy.* He did not respond. She continued to call him. He felt humiliated. He kicked the horse. Startled, the horse jumped. Barman rode his horse quickly away from the house. He could still hear her voice clearly, but he decided to ignore it. He passed through the leafy vegetation; tall stalks brushed against his shoulders. Riding away on his horse, he wanted to chase after something: freedom. Then he remembered Humam.

He imagined Humam's face in front of him. His lighted house stood in the distance under the shelter of some trees. The first time he had seen the house, the walls glistened white against a background of greenery, but this was no longer the case: he could see that moss had overtaken the walls. Barman could no longer wait to see his old friend. Humam was the only person Barman could speak with on this mountain. Even though Barman had just spent time with him a few days ago when they walked and fished together, Humam was still a puzzle. That man was always fishing for Barman's uneasiness, challenging him to think; but Barman knew that he could not escape from him.

The house was covered with vines that crept up to the roof, where there were piles of dead flowers and leaves. The door was like the mouth of a cave hidden deep beneath encroaching foliage. If the windows were opened, they would let in tree branches. There was trash everywhere. *Ah, the old man had become lazy again.* Barman let his horse loose to graze on the grass at a distance from the house. He called. His voice reverberated from tree to tree. He was surprised to hear his voice echo through the trees around him.

Birds flew off the rooftop as he approached the house. He could see some of the dry leaves stir, disturbed by the flurry of birds. *How different this was from his house. Poppy had made his house a model of cleanliness.* He imagined Poppy's graceful hands sweeping the yard as she sang, her soft, fresh voice floating in the surrounding trees. Like the singing of magical fairies!

Barman knocked on the door to Humam's house as he peered in through the glass. He could see only his own face and the reflections of the trees behind him, so he blocked the light with his hands.

Barman could see Humam sprawled on a chair. He appeared to be sleeping soundly. Barman wanted to bother him. He would wake the old man up and pepper him with questions, as Humam had once done to him. The door opened easily. Barman tiptoed in. He wanted to surprise Humam. Barman would wake him up and then he would throw a question at him. Barman would ask: Are you happy? Then Humam would open his eyes. Yes, that is what he would do. Barman trembled with excitement, thinking about this wonderful game that they would soon play. A snippet of long-buried joy would pop out. Barman knew that this was a child's game, but there was a difference between grandfathers and grandchildren. *Just do whatever you like! Just do it!*

"Hey!" He touched Humam.

There was no response. Humam did not move.

Barman touched him. He touched him again. Then Barman examined the old body on the chair. He lifted the hand. It was cold! *Oh no!* He couldn't believe it. He shouted Humam's name. But even though he shouted several times, Humam did not reply. The old man had died. Barman peered at Humam's face. Humam was smiling!

4

B arman tried to reconstruct how Humam had died. How strange it was! The old man remained calm, his nerves under control. Just for a moment he felt strange about this death, then he proceeded to act carefully and consciously, as if something like this happened to him every day. First, he went outside, called his horse and then he left the house. He worried that ants would surround the corpse or that wolves would venture out of the overgrown grass on the hill and devour the body.

It did not take him long to reach the marketplace. At the first stall that he encountered he asked for a sheet of white paper, then he looked around for a pole. He saw the market groundskeeper sweeping trash with a long-handled broom made of the ribs of coconut fronds. He patted the man on his back and pointed to the broom. Barman pulled out one long wisp. Puzzled, the groundskeeper watched him closely. Barman went into a store and asked for a bit of glue. In a short while, he had assembled a white paper flag, which he waved while sitting atop his horse. With a loud trembling voice, he announced the death.

"My friends, an exemplary human being has departed our earth!"

He tried to repeat the sentence several times.

People ran out from food stalls, shops, and buses, and gathered around him. They asked who had died, where, when, what happened? But Barman only repeated his announcement. Disturbed by the crowd, his horse shied and snorted. Barman tried to calm him down, but the horse reared and bucked repeatedly. Barman fell off the horse. Women screamed as they backed away. They could hear the horse kicking a pile of empty cans. Barman lay sprawled on the road in front of the market. He was still mumbling his announcement. The white flag in his hand was torn and trampled beneath many feet. The people around him kept asking him what had happened. Barman continued to shout, hoarse and weary. The market groundskeeper tried to explain to the crowd.

"It's like this… Like this… Someone has died. Someone has died!"

"Who?"

"I don't know, but someone has died!"

When the crowd turned to him, Barman could no longer hear anything.

"Wait until he recovers," someone said.

"Let's lift him up! Watch out for his feet! His head!"

Several men lifted Barman. It was chaotic. The seam of his shirt tore. Several strands of his white hair had fallen loose and were trampled on. They laid Barman down in a food stall on a pile of cabbages. The men who had carried him there tried to move his arms. Just a few people were left. Those who returned to check on him kept saying, "Poor man." "Tsk, tsk."

The market activities resumed. Sounds of vehicles on the road could be heard again. Passengers inside the buses waved to the people on the street before they were whisked away. The vegetable vendor tried to sell the cabbages that were under Barman. Before bargaining for the cabbages, the women buyers glanced at Barman and asked, "What was he saying?" The vendor shook his head and asked how many kilograms of cabbages they needed.

The aged body lay sprawled out over the cabbages. The groundskeeper waited patiently. He was waiting for Barman to move. He sprinkled water from a coconut shell bowl on to Barman's forehead. He felt for Barman's breath. Then the groundskeeper unbuttoned Barman's soiled shirt and rubbed water on to his chest. The market people pestered him with questions: "What did he say?" "Who died?" Death, death! People asked each other—anyone and even themselves—was there anyone in their family who was ill? Who could ever guarantee that only the ill would die? Even the market people knew that anyone could die at any moment.

An old woman, a seller of flower offerings, went to the groundskeeper and insisted, "Wake him up now. Ask him who died!"

The groundskeeper sprinkled more water on Barman. "As if your own life depended on it..." he grumbled to the woman.

The woman offered him a packet of flower offerings—red, white, yellow, and green.

"Use this!"

He opened the packet and scattered the flower petals and leaves evenly along the length of Barman's body. The old man was covered with flower petals. Several men and women approached the stall and tried to help. The women scattered more flowers. Children holding slingshots squatted close by, watching. Suddenly a man chased them all away, swearing, telling them that this was not a show. The children just shifted their positions or moved slightly away. The old man lay unconscious, wet and covered with flowers! The cabbage seller warned the children to be careful and not to step on his vegetables. When Barman began to move, whispers spread through the crowd. Several more people gathered around the stall.

Then Barman regained consciousness. He moved his head and stretched his arms and legs. The flower petals slipped off his head. He wiped his forehead. Drops of water dripped from his beard. He realized that he was in the midst of a crowd. He shivered and he flexed his hands. The groundskeeper straightened Barman's clothes and re-buttoned his shirt. Barman looked around.

"Where am I?" he asked.

"Here," said the groundskeeper.

"Where?"

"In the market."

"On earth?"

That was an odd question. Everyone was silent. Several children giggled. The groundskeeper shot a look at the children.

"Yes, on earth," someone said.

Several people mumbled. *Where else would he be if not on earth, hmm?* But someone shushed the crowd and they grew quiet again. Barman looked first at the groundskeeper, then at the crowd around and above him. He looked all around.

"I'm a stranger here," he said.

"No, sir. You're amongst friends," said the groundskeeper.

"No. I am a stranger everywhere. A stranger!"

The crowd let him stand up. A few people stretched out their hands as if to keep him from falling down again. Barman straightened his clothes. He picked off a flower petal that had stuck to his trousers. He smelled it. With the small white blossom in his hand, he looked at the people surrounding him, one by one. Cabbages, the food stall that was constructed from bamboo, and all of the people. There were so many people gathered around him.

"What happened?" asked Barman.

There was no answer.

"Where's my horse?"

The people in the crowd looked around.

"The horse, the horse," they said. "Where is it?"

But no one moved. Barman looked down at the ground. Suddenly he straightened up and he looked directly at the crowd.

"Friends. A true human being has left our earth."

The voice rang out clearly in the midst of silence. People gathered around and stared at him.

"Who left?"

"Who died?"

The people pushed forward, closer so that they could hear him better.

"Not died!" Barman insisted.

"What then?"

"His heart stopped. He's leaning against the chair. Cold. No longer breathing."

"Dead. Dead," said many people in the crowd. They shrugged their shoulders.

"Ask him where it happened."

"Where? Where?" asked many people.

Barman was silent for a moment.

"Follow me," he said.

Barman stepped forward. The groundskeeper was the first to follow him. An old man, the night watchman, touched the groundskeeper's shoulder. He said:

"I saw his eyes. His eyes."

"What?"

"That man is different from all of us." Then he followed Barman closely, almost touching his back. The groundskeeper was behind him. A crowd formed. They left the market. Who was not touched by death? The market quickly became deserted. Twenty-three men were sent to escort Barman on his journey. The women followed them to the edge of the market and then returned to attend to their merchandise. The bus passengers who were about to leave stretched their heads out of the windows. A taxi driver got out of his car and stood next to his vehicle.

When he got to the side of the road, Barman stopped. His horse was grazing near the road. He called it by name. The horse looked up. It took one more mouthful of grass and sauntered over to Barman. The animal rubbed its head against Barman. Everyone watched them.

"Get on," the groundskeeper suggested.

"Yes, get on!" urged people in the crowd.

The people lifted Barman on to the horse's back. Barman felt weary. He sat on the horse and held on to the horse's mane. His entire body was listless, but he was happy to be on the horse where he could rest.

"It's a long journey," he said to the people who helped him.

"We're coming along," the people replied.

He could finally relax. Sitting on the horse with his legs extended, he could release his exhaustion. Weariness flowed down and out through his limbs. For the first time in his entire life, he was being escorted by many people while he was riding his horse. He recalled images of bridegrooms in the past who rode horses and wore fancy hats. But he did not want to be compared to a bridegroom. He was seventy-six years old. He felt strange. The image of grandeur excited him. He gazed at the panorama around him: mountain, valley, verdant trees. And the crowd! His pounding heart warmed his body. He looked about in amazement at this unprecedented scene. His senses were revived. He sat majestically astride his horse, a pure white horse. He rubbed his feet against the horse's belly and the creature raised its tail. The group moved slowly forward.

People came out of the houses along the edge of the road to watch the procession. Other travelers on the road stopped and watched the entourage pass. They quietly shuffled forward, heading to greet the death that had taken place somewhere else. Sweat began to soak through their clothes. The sun, high in the sky, round, pulsating. Barman felt comfortable on the horse. He felt that everything was just as it should be. They were silent, walking, directly under the sun. The mountain air softened the sunrays.

Barman was at peace astride the horse—but whenever he tried to reconstruct in his mind what had happened, he always missed something. He had to admit that he was very happy that day. He could not explain why. He was riding his horse; dozens of people were escorting him. They followed him so obediently. This was a dream that had been hidden deep in his heart. Ah, he felt grand! It seemed as if this was a journey to eternity!

The walk was quicker than a casual stroll. The entourage kept up with the horse. Mountain people walk quickly. Barman's shirt was stiff with dried sweat. He began to feel warm. They traveled a well-trodden path through grass and overgrowth, weaving around hillocks.

The group stopped when Barman, who was in the lead, stopped suddenly, sitting alertly on his horse. There were two men coming down the path. They stopped when Barman signaled them. They were carrying something on a stretcher, something covered with a cloth, something long. Barman looked at the stretcher. He began to tremble. The people gathered around him so that he would not fall.

"Come here! Come here!" said Barman, with his last ounce of strength.

He urged his horse closer to the stretcher and bent down to lift the cloth. It was a corpse! The two men tried to evade him, but the crowd had blocked the road. In the midst of the overgrown grass, under the midday sun, the world seemed to stop. The crowd waited. Barman continued to inspect the body.

"Who are you?" he asked the two men.

"We're employees of the City Coroner's Office," one of the men replied while taking out a piece of paper. Barman looked at the letter.

"Where are you taking him?"

"To the cemetery."

Barman was quiet. Several thoughts buzzed through his mind. He weakened; people held him steady. Death was a puzzle for him! He did not understand how Humam had died! This was extraordinary! Who informed the City about his death? No one else knew about it.

"Who told you about this?"

"We were just ordered to pick up this body."

"You cannot do this."

The two men shrugged their shoulders and the corpse they were carrying was jostled a little. Then they signaled the crowd to stand aside. The crowd parted for them.

"No! No!" shouted Barman.

"Issue a complaint at the coroner's office," they replied.

Barman was stunned. The men bearing the stretcher were already off in the distance. The crowd stared at Barman quizzically. They looked at him, then they turned to look at the stretcher-bearers. Barman did not move. He just gazed in the direction of the carriers. He just watched them. His eyes grew big and hard. His body tensed, twisted. The people helped him to descend from the horse. The two stretcher-bearers were no longer visible; they had disappeared beyond the overgrown grass. The crowd was anxious, but not one person opened his mouth. Barman tried to speak. They waited. Barman pointed in the direction where the two men had gone.

"A true human being! A teacher!" He couldn't say anything more. Someone caught his horse and brought it to him. The crowd signaled to each other and helped Barman back up on his horse. Someone gave the horse a shove. No one knew where it should go, but the horse began to walk. The crowd just followed it. With Barman hunched over on his horse, not caring about the journey, the horse sought its own path. The crowd continued to follow the horse. No one asked any questions; it seemed as if this was the right thing to do. They walked briskly. The horse stopped in front of a house. They knocked on the door. Several people helped Barman down from the horse and carried him to the door. From inside the house, Poppy could see them carrying Barman. Quickly, she opened the door.

"Papa!" Immediately, Poppy calmed down and prepared to receive him.

"Poppy," said Barman weakly.

The people carried Barman into the house. Poppy asked them to lay him down on the sofa in the living room. Poppy quickly began to tend to Barman. She hurried to the back of the house. People were still standing in the doorway, on the terrace, in the yard. Poppy returned with towels to wipe the old man's body with warm water. When she realized that the people who had brought him home were still there, she thanked them. Then they left, leaving silence behind. When they were at a distance from the house, they began to speak. Their voices snuck under the shade of the trees. Their faint whispers, timid and secretive, quickly settled into the vegetation along the road and down the mountainside. The twenty-three men did not understand what had just happened.

Poppy wiped Barman's soiled face and hands. She did not ask the old man any questions.

"I've already told you, Papa. You are not safe outside the house."

She prattled on to Barman about his health, about not eating on time, about the scorching sun, about the long journey, about imposing on other people. Poppy was not pleased that Barman still needed other people. She ordered him to lie down in their room and went out to search for the horse. She quickly led the horse into its stall. She went into the house and closed the doors and fastened them so that the old man would not be able to leave. Now that she was busy, she felt restored and happy to be working.

Poppy did not ask the people what had happened to Barman, and the old man did not want to tell her anything. What happened outside the house was not her concern.

Alone in his room, Barman stared at the ceiling. He was confused. The boundary between dream and reality had become fuzzy. The chain of events that had unfolded that day slipped below his consciousness. The only thing that was still fresh in his memory was the ride to the market. Everything that had happened after that was a jumble of dream, memory, and reality. His world was hazy. He stared at vague, gray images on the ceiling. He could recall cabbages, the crowd, and the people who had brought him home. That journey home stirred new thoughts. *Where were those people now? Were they still milling about the marketplace? I miss them. I've lost something. Who was it? Humam! O, poor noble Humam!*

The old man wept. He could not understand Humam's departure and the way he left. Now Barman wanted to cry for his old friend. Perhaps there was no one else who would weep for him. How pathetic it would be if a person died without anyone caring for him. By weeping, he felt closer to Humam. The faces of the two men who had been carrying Humam's body were cold and uncaring. Barman had once seen men carrying the carcass of a horse from a road; the faces of those men were similar to the faces of the men who had been carrying Humam. It was the strangest death he had witnessed. He stopped crying. Was it right for him to cry about everything? Perhaps Humam had intentionally chosen his path. Perhaps sorrow was not the appropriate reaction for his death. *Humam, what did you mean by this?* Barman could picture Humam smiling! This made him more confused. If he could have avoided it, Barman would have preferred never to have met Humam. He felt very old and very confused. Perhaps philosophy or psychology could explain this event, but he had always hated social science. He was depressed. He could disregard death, but the puzzle of Humam's choice was so disturbing! Barman would surely curse the old man if he ever met him again. This was too much! Of course, he could not ask Poppy and Bobby or Dosy for their opinions about this. *I don't want to involve any of you in this puzzle, Bob, Dos, Poppy. Bobby only thinks about "what could be more beautiful than living with a beautiful woman who serves you loyally."* That boy was just like himself in his youth.

In another room, Poppy was busy preparing something for him. *Know this, Poppy. Inside this room I am alone, lonely, abandoned, isolated from everyone. I'm a pathetic old man.* He wiped his stinging eyes when he heard Poppy's footsteps approach his room.

In the morning, a man wearing a woven straw hat and carrying a briefcase full of papers knocked on the door. He searched for a nameplate on the wall. He knocked again. Poppy opened the door. She was not expecting anyone. Indeed, she did not know anyone here. Her world on this mountain was one of complete freedom. The man at the door asked for someone named Barman. *Who knew that Barman was here?* Bobby's acquaintances had all kept this place a secret so that the house was truly free from any kind of business. "It is your world, Poppy, filled only with Papa," Bobby had said. Poppy did not have any business with anyone. She did not have any debts nor did she leave money with anyone. There was no reason for any government office to contact them on this mountain. Indeed, this was Barman's house, but Bobby had taken care of all official business.

The man explained that he was a housing official. This was a matter of inheritance that had to be settled with Barman.

"It's good news, ma'am."

The officer explained that Barman had inherited a house from someone. From Humam. Poppy did not know that name. She examined the documents. It was true! She wondered if she should telephone Bobby or just tell Barman. She asked Barman to come out to meet with the officer. Poppy asked him if he had any relatives named Humam. Barman shook his head, but he said that there was nothing strange on the face of this earth and that anything was possible. Poppy did not understand what he meant, but she didn't want to ask him to explain it. She quickly disappeared to the back of the house.

"Yes, I am his beneficiary," said Barman.

The officer asked him to sign the documents. Barman obediently signed the papers, as if it was the only thing he could do.

Poppy saw a sudden change in Barman after the officer left. He smiled gently as he had in previous days.

"Tell me, Papa, what do you want?"

Barman said that he wanted to live in Humam's house. Poppy objected. They had to live together in their own home. Bobby had decided on this house for them.

"No, Poppy. I will tell Bobby!"

That's impossible! Poppy would fight for this house, for Barman's life, and for her life. If one thing changed, then everything would change, so she would resist any kind of change. Her life on this mountain would be useless; she could imagine a disastrous ending. Her daring decision would be wasted. But Barman insisted that he was going to live in that house. The decision could not be delayed any longer. *You live in this house, Poppy.* She argued that he wanted a separation, which she did not want. *No, Poppy. That is not what I want.*

If that was what Barman wanted, then that was what he would do. Barman wanted to be alone. That house had captured his attention. *I am not responsible for him outside of this house*, Poppy said to herself. Barman was not asking for Poppy's permission to leave, but he felt that he had to tell her of his decision because she was responsible to Bobby. He imagined a cave. That white house was like a cave, surrounded by leaves from the ground to the roof. He felt invigorated. Poppy was good to him. She helped him to pack his warm clothing. He promised to return for meals. *This will only be temporary, Poppy. I am not abandoning you.*

He carried his suitcase to the door. Poppy went with him. The horse was brought out of its stall and the suitcase was lifted onto the horse's back. Then he got on the horse.

From atop the horse, he said, "It's that white house there near the tall trees."

Barman straightened his hat, patted the horse's neck and squeezed his legs against the horse's belly. The horse began to trot. Poppy stood in the yard. She just stood there. She did not say good-bye to Barman. Barman spurred the horse on. He remembered rolling in the grass with Poppy when they had just arrived. His passion had peaked when he was sitting next to her and felt her soft flesh. That memory tortured him. That was why he wanted to be free of that woman and now he was riding away on his horse. *Your possessions are your chains*, Humam had said.

At a distance from the house, he slowed his horse down to a steady walk. The horse used this opportunity to pull at the overgrown grass along the path. How happy Barman was now. *He would live in own house. He would still see Poppy occasionally; that would be all right. He did have to eat. Or he could make his own meals like Humam had. He probably would not be able to do that, at least not just yet, as he did not know how to live by himself yet. Was he brave enough? Yes, now he felt free.* He took a deep breath, filling his chest with cold air. *This is freedom!*

Poppy was still standing in front of the door when Barman was far down the path.

"As you wish, Papa," she said. "I have done my job. Now you do yours. Even if you are not here, you are the symbol of my love for this life, nothing more."

She closed the door, but she surprised herself at how loudly the door slammed shut. She lay down on the bed. She didn't know why her eyes were damp. She didn't know why.

The journey to Humam's house on horseback was quick. The horse already knew the twists and turns of the mountain's paths. Barman was like a doll hanging onto the horse's mane, swaying from side to side. Humam's house, like the other mountain houses, was quiet, covered with vines. *Immersed in secrets*, thought Barman, *like life itself. Ah, Humam left his house to me.* He had not expected it, of course. However, he was intrigued. Humam had transformed a worthless house into something miraculous, grand and amazing. As he neared Humam's house Barman felt as if he were entering into mist and this delighted him. *This is strange.* He tried to shape his thoughts, but it was useless. He decided to not think about the past few days. *Ah, Poppy had taught him something.* He was embarrassed about that woman. *Let it be. Humam's perplexing death... perhaps he was still leaning against the chair.* No, his eyes were not wrong. Humam had departed without any ceremony, prayers or burial. *Did the City Coroner's people really bury him and not take his corpse to the hospital to be cut up and used for science?* Barman decided that he would learn from Humam, the model of an old man who was decisive, but secretive. *Humam was an exemplary human being! That man had determined everything about his life, even his own death. He was the victor!* Barman smiled. He no longer had any doubts about Humam's death. Humam had surely wanted to die. Barman entered the house with a peaceful resignation. He no longer wanted to search for Humam's grave. Barman accepted his death. He swept aside the remains of fish bones and dry rice in the kitchen. *That Humam!*

Barman took his suitcase into the bedroom. As he examined the closets, he felt an affinity with Humam's fate. How similar they were. *I am Humam who is still alive.* There were many other aspects of Humam that Barman hoped were still fresh and healthy. Sitting on the chair where Humam had sat, Barman briefly recalled his friend's face. Then he recalled the faces of Poppy, Dosy, Bobby, and his grandchildren. They were all there, miles away, beyond reach. Even though Poppy symbolized disappointment, he always thought about her, especially when he thought about food. Who else would feed him? But he dreamed that he would gradually free himself completely from her. He wanted to be just as independent as Humam had been. Surely Humam had been happy with his life and his death. Barman wanted to be like that. But this thought startled him. He did not just want to become someone else. In the past, long before this, he had wanted to live independently. *Humam had affected him too much. No. Yes.* He felt something creeping through his head, a dull pain. *Don't think, Papa, live as well as you can.* An image of Poppy appeared before him. *No, noooo!*

Barman did not make any rules in his new house. He let the spiders weave their webs anywhere—on the ceilings and the hanging lampshades, over the cabinets. Dust gathered everywhere. The horse was no longer kept in a stable; it roamed freely. But the horse just grazed nearby, under the shade of the trees to escape from the blazing hot sun. There was dung everywhere; the grass flourished. What had Humam done every day? Fish? Flex his muscles? In that house far up on the mountainside where no one knew him, Barman felt that there was no longer any use for philosophical truths.

His most important job was to throw himself down on the sofa. Stare at the ceiling. Empty his brain. *Emptying the mind is the beginning of peacefulness. But... curses!* Just as he had begun to feel peaceful, he heard a sound at the door. Someone was knocking at the door. Barman looked out. He seemed to know the person.

"It's you, isn't it?"

"Yes, I've met you before."

Now he remembered. This was one of the men who had carried Humam down the mountain.

"There's nothing else that needs to be taken care of!"

The officer took his notes out of his briefcase. He held a neatly typed document. The man showed the paper to Barman, but the old man refused to read it.

"I don't read any more. I don't have any use for letters," he said.

"This is a statement," said the officer, "that explains that a corpse has been taken away from this place."

"No. No."

The man asked him to sign the statement so that he could close the file. It was a statement from the cemetery that a man by the name of Humam had been buried there. The officer placed the paper on the table. Barman refused to read it, so the man read it to him.

"This is proof that the job has been executed as promised."

"There was no promise. There is no one who will complain, believe me."

Barman sent the officer away. The man left the house, but he stood in the yard for a rather long time. The officer had disturbed Barman's thoughts. Now Barman was reminded of Humam and his death. He wanted to ask about Humam's grave. *But, why? No, that wouldn't be necessary.* Barman had already sent away the officer who may have given him an explanation. Ah, at times like this, he wanted a glass of wine. Poppy would have served it to him. *Poppyyyyy!*

The officer did not leave the premises. He made sketches and notes. Scratches. Then he returned to the wall of the house and took out from his briefcase a brush and a bottle of paste. He pasted a sheet of paper onto the wall of the house. Barman watched him, but he did not do anything. Then the man shoved a piece of paper under the door and left. Barman tried to ignore the paper under the door, but a puff of wind blew it into the house.

As he crossed the room, Barman stepped on the piece of paper. Without thinking, he picked it up. He eyes glanced at the neatly written letters. There was a sentence written across the top of the paper: "Inform us when you are going to die." His eyes popped open! He read the sentence several times. Perhaps his vision had blurred. *That's very odd. No, that is indeed what's written here.* He gripped the paper tightly as he paced back and forth in the house. He memorized it. Perhaps this is what had happened to Humam. He imagined Humam's face in every corner in the house. Then he examined his own face in the glass door. A dim image of Humam's face was there as well. "Inform us when you are going to die." He felt very old now. Weak and weary, he lay down on the sofa, still gripping the paper.

He was famished. He had already eaten up all the food in the house. He thought of Poppy. He had not seen her for two days. Early one morning he had woken up with an empty stomach. Poppy floated into his thoughts. When he went out of his bedroom, he saw containers of food set on the table. This food was surely from Poppy! She had sent him food. Ah, he hoped that Poppy had not walked over to his house in the middle of the night or in the early morning just to bring him food. He wanted very much to meet with his beloved.

He thought of his horse. He could no longer restrain his desire. Poppy had done something for him. He headed for his old house, leaving the containers behind. It was a cold morning on the mountain; he huddled in a thick jacket. The chilly air seemed to shout out about his freedom. He stopped beneath a tree and gazed at his old house. Poppy was there. *Is that house a haven of freedom or a prison?* Before he could answer his own question, his horse brought him closer to the house.

"Poppy, you have worked so hard," he said.

"I enjoy it, Papa."

"Don't do this again, my dear."

"I'm worried that you're hungry, Papa. I don't want that."

Barman looked at the young woman. Her eyes were glistening, as if they held tears.

"It's not necessary. Because… " but he could not continue his sentence.

"Why, Papa?"

"I'm not always at home!"

Contrary to what Barman feared, Poppy smiled.

"I suspected that. I know. You want to avoid me. Not just me; you want to avoid everything. Even yourself, if that's possible. Everything. But you can't do that. We must live with other people. With other people, not just by ourselves."

These thoughts were very meaningful. Poppy was the only woman that Barman admired.

Barman stayed with Poppy for awhile. They talked about the horse, the weather, insects. He wanted to show Poppy that he was happy with his new situation. He firmly requested her to not bother to prepare his meals. If he did not come to her, that meant that he had enough food. Barman kissed Poppy as he took his leave. The horse waited for him outside. There was still plenty of fresh grass for grazing. The grass was as green as it had ever been, the flowers in the garden as well. *I like to remember you in the white dress, like the sun strolling amongst the flowers. Even though you prefer the flowered-patterned dress, I'll always remember you in this way.*

When Barman was on the horse, Poppy said, "Papa, you are a strange man!"

Barman only laughed. *Exactly*, he thought. Barman rode the horse through the flower garden. Slowly, he picked a bud, then he turned to look at Poppy. Poppy understood. She approached him. She felt sad. This was not the way for people to make love. She accepted the flower from Barman, then Barman kissed her hand. She didn't know why, but she felt that something was not right. *What is it with you, old Barman?* She let him go. When the old man had gone a distance, she dropped the flower. She felt uneasy. The flower fell to the grass. It was white. She wanted to cry, but she restrained herself. She forced herself to feel happy, then she returned to the house and closed the door as if nothing had happened.

Barman contemplated his situation. He wanted to understand the meaning of his life. It seemed as if he could still converse with Humam. A man as old as him surely could relay much wisdom. *Do you still like to fish in your new world, Humam?* Barman tried to understand the path that Humam had taken. The path to live and the path to stop living. He admired Humam more than the books he had read—the Talmud, the Bible, the Qur'an, *Das Capital*, biographies of important people, film stars. Humam was born to live in his own way. How magnificent he was; his courage knew no fear. Barman wanted to be born again, to pave a path towards something new in his life. He knew that he was old, and this realization encouraged him to search for something important. Something that other people did not have, but that he would have. Humam seized his thoughts. No, he did not want to be exactly like Humam. He had his own peculiarities. Barman admired Humam, but he wanted to be free of his friend as well. He wanted to live a life of independence. He imagined himself sitting alone in the middle of a crowd of people, as he had done in the city. People unknown to each other, not greeting each other. A crowd of mutes. He tried to understand the universe on his own terms. He accepted his solitude.

All this time, he lay alone in his room. If he wanted to eat, he signaled his horse to take him to Poppy. In accordance with his request, she no longer took food to him. Barman would go to her when he needed her. He no longer spoke at the dining table or while Poppy packed his food. She did not feel it was necessary to say anything either. They sat at the table, picking at the food, without needing to converse. Everything went smoothly, like a well-oiled machine. When he was finished, Barman would rise to leave quietly. The woman opened the door, closed it again. He would whistle for his horse. When his horse approached, he would mount it and ride to his new home.

During that time he tried to make sense of his life. He did not like writing down his thoughts. He realized that he would repeat himself and go around in circles. *Let it be; this is not a search for knowledge, but a journey to wisdom.* How serenely happy he was! Perfect isolation! He smiled. Down at the foot of the mountain, it was a world of noise, a world of a soulless crowd. But here, there was radiant light! He imagined that he was a single firefly flitting about in the rice fields in the dark. He liked that image. His memories of fireflies in the rice fields were ethereal. Yes, I am that firefly! Solitary, but never tiring of twinkling!

5

One evening, Barman paced back and forth in the front room, maneuvering between the chairs. Darkness had settled on the mountain, but moonlight filtered through the spaces between the leaves that covered the house and the glass panes in the door. Now that he had freed himself from his beloved, he felt that something had changed. The woman was a beautiful, fascinating memory. He often thought about her at night when he was alone in bed. Poppy with her perfect beauty came to him as an angel as if she were a creature of light, untouchable but exquisitely beautiful. *Ah, how graceful she was!* He always thought of her as an angel from his dreams. He smiled at her over the dining table. He allowed Poppy to do as she wished, as if she were a dream that should be savored. He was gentle with his beloved and she was gentle with him, all without any exchange of words. This was a new life!

He noticed the moonlight shining into the house. He knew that his horse was waiting in the yard. The horse was used to sleeping on the grass or taking shelter in the overgrowth. When he opened the door, the horse would rise up from its resting place and approach him while snorting gently. Barman stood up and looked out through the gaps between the leaves on the vines. It was pitch black beneath a clump of trees, but there was a blaze of yellow moonlight on the open field. He had a sudden desire to find some night action. Why would he close himself up in his room on such a magical night as this? It would truly be a foolish thing to do. He was free now. It was so beautiful outside, so breathtakingly beautiful. He wanted to go outside. Unlike other people who were tucked away in their homes, he wanted to go out to absorb the beauty of the night, which would then radiate from within him. His happiness glowed like the brightness of the moon. The mountain, like him, was vast, boundless, expansive, and majestic. There was something new inside him—beauty or happiness or freshness or freedom—he didn't know what. It made him smile. After wrestling with it, he had won the war against his restlessness. He had overcome the struggle in his own way. The solitude around him brought him back to life because he had accepted its presence in his life.

He listened to the sounds of the night. Ground animals, bats, even falling leaves! The ubiquitous mountain pine trees caught the wind and threw languid sounds far into the distance, turning them into the whispers of magical night creatures. The sounds were heartbreaking. Solitude. Barman yearned for that solitude. *It is you, the one that I have yearned for!* He made his peace with the night. No longer did he hit his head, moan, or hold his breath. Time had taught him that victory would eventually be his. This was the day he had been waiting for, the day of his release. His burdens had been thrown aside; time had dissolved into eternity. He befriended the universe. The moon, pine trees, animals, and his horse. *Oh, yes, where is that horse?* At that moment he caught a glimpse of the white horse walking majestically under the shimmering yellow moonlight. Its coat looked whiter to him. The white coat glistened in the darkness of the night. He shivered; he felt intoxicated and clutched his chest. His heart was throbbing lightly; he felt as if he were floating. He wanted to catch his horse.

Hurriedly, he snatched up his wool jacket from the sofa and put it on. He realized that he was much thinner than he had been. It was true. He was thin, wrinkled, tall; his hair was white and his beard had lengthened. But he felt strong and his eyes sparkled. He put on a *peci* cap, such as Muslim men wore. It would protect him from the cold. Tonight he would go out and commune with the night.

He opened the door; it creaked. His horse whinnied and the leaves in the grove of trees rustled. It seemed as if the horse's whinny echoed throughout the entire mountain. The other sounds of the night stopped. There was only the sound of his footsteps. The horse swished its tail and bowed as Barman approached. Moonlight snuck in between the dark shadows. There were pockets of darkness and light all around him. Barman mounted his horse. He sat tall on the horse's back. His eyesight was sharper than the moonlight. *Ah, his heart was pounding. Tonight he would do something important. This was a sign, his pounding heart.*

At first, he just rode around the yard. Then he stopped beneath the moon, beneath the open sky. The moonlight penetrated deep into his body. In a golden haze, he sat upright on his horse, like a statue of a god guarding the mountain. He gazed towards the shimmering electric lights in the distance. That was the market. *Yes, I miss them. They had been happy to welcome me during the day. Why don't I visit them now?* They were all, as he was, parts of something bigger, that is, humanity. In his new home, he had a chance to think about what was missing from his life. He might find some of those missing elements amongst the people in the marketplace. *Where were they tonight?* He recalled the smell of cabbages.

Before he realized it, the horse began walking slowly down the mountain slope. He let the animal take him. Even animals have desires, don't they? He enjoyed the swaying of the horse's stride, the soft sighs of the pine trees, the yellow moonlight on the mountain.

The houses on the mountainside were stacked silently, with lamps that were meant to light up the surroundings. Barman did not like the people of those houses. They were living here trying to forget the world, while he was searching for something. His journey this time, and every time, was the journey of humanity in search of something.

There was the bus station, the market, the lights. Ah, perhaps he would escort Poppy to the market again. No, she was sleeping now. He felt love for the woman who was sleeping soundly in a white dress, with a peaceful radiant face. *Sleep, my dear. Here am I, guarding the world that has drowned in darkness.* His old house was over in the distance, on the field splashed with the moonlight. Poppy, who always welcomed him home, was there, sound asleep. If she declared unbounded love for him, kissed him, caressed him, even released her passions with him, he would accept her and thank her. That was love. And what was better than love? He could now accept Poppy's love, which had seemed strange to him a short time ago. She had given him everything he asked for, but now he asked her only to stay in the house so that Bobby would not take charge of him again.

Everything would change if his son tried to take over and manage things for him. That son of his would say anything to defend his own opinion. And that would mess things up. He hoped Bobby would understand. Barman did not need anything anymore, except peace, which he now had achieved. At that moment, the field was very clear. *Where did the mist go?* Even the mist knew that this night was just for Barman. More than at any other time in his life, Barman had fallen in love with nature. As for Poppy, every time he thought of the woman, he called her "my pretty angel" in his heart. This was the purest kind of love. It was time for an old man like him to live honestly, purely, simply, and unpretentiously. He had freed himself from everything that could possibly interfere with the purity of his love for her. *If we do not desire anything from our possessions, then we are truly free.*

Barman wanted to go to the market. *What was happening there, on this meaningful night? Were the market people gathering, bargaining for their merchandise, guarding the cabbages? Of course not.* He wondered what happened at the market at night. Deserted, there would be dogs wandering about sniffing for scraps of meat, their snouts sifting through the dirt, whimpering. The studs chasing the bitches. *What kind of silence sliced through the bustle of the daytime market? Where were the people who were weary and asleep? Where were the dogs who, after feasting on scraps and mating, also fell asleep? Was that what their life was like? What humiliation! Surely they were sleepy and unthinking.* Poppy had advised him to not think. She was right. But the decision to stop thinking had to be conscious and conclusive. This took courage. To stop thinking out of desperation was an act of cowardice. Barman wanted to make a courageous, conscientious decision. He had almost hit his head against a wall in desperation. But he had been able to free himself and find what he was searching for.

And just what was he searching for? Just a moment, the definitive conclusion about eternal life cannot be formulated in a sentence. It can only be expressed in a fully victorious smile. In the savoring of the moonlight. In peaceful friendship with nature. In nights that are clothed in both darkness and light. The mountainside transformed into new life. Atop his horse, Barman felt small, but significant. Fireflies flitting about in the middle of the night! They did not fly about in a group, but by themselves, individually. The solitude was mesmerizing. The horse beneath him seemed to understand what he was thinking; this was sublime happiness. The horse ambled forward slowly.

The moonlight beamed down over the bus stop, enhancing the light of the electric lamps. In the areas where there were no lamps, the moonlight melted through the darkness. *Life at this station has stopped,* thought Barman when he saw trucks lined up on the asphalt. He wanted to speak with someone here, anyone. He wanted to say something. *Living in ignorance like this is a sin. People are unwisely busy throughout the day, bustling back and forth, and throwing away their lives every single day. That is a sin, my children.* The horse stepped lightly on the asphalt at the bus station. Evenly, like the sound of a well-oiled machine. They stopped next to a pole with an electric lamp. There was a bit of haze around the light above his head. The market stalls, shops, food stands; everything was drowned in stony silence.

Barman listened for the sound of someone breathing. He would wake that person up and talk to him in the middle of the night. Perhaps there was someone here whom he had met. His horse carried him in his search, step by step. *Yes, there. There was someone asleep! Someone huddled in a sarong, asleep on the sidewalk in front of a store. Was this the fruitless life that he had cursed?* Barman approached the sleeping man. He smiled bitterly. *What kind of indignity lay wrapped up fast asleep in that bundle of cloth?* There was a dog shivering in the cold near the sleeping man. *What was the difference between them?* He slipped down from the horse. The moon threw shadows down at his feet. The horse's steps sounded on the gravel. *Every movement in this life, every moment of silence in this life, was to be savored,* Humam had taught him that. The simplicity of the market buildings pleased him. He inhaled the silence; it was enthralling, even the most deserted areas of the market.

Barman gazed for a long time at the person asleep on the storefront terrace. *Ignorance in the silence of the night. The harshness of humanity is the curse of life.* True, perhaps these people were now liberated from their daily activities and had forgotten their lives of suffering, but when they woke up, they would resume chasing life. They would be perpetually chasing life. They were caught in machines that revolved constantly. Machines! Barman was terrified of that thought. Even though he had seen it in his beloved Poppy. "Don't think, Papa," the woman had said. He had hated that woman once. But perhaps Poppy had made her decision. *Poppy, his beautiful angel that he loved now, not because of the wine and food she served him or because of her gentleness.* He loved her for her integrity. *And, ah, her humble way of sleeping.*

Serenity was good only if it was rooted in wisdom. These friends who were asleep now had bothered his thoughts. He recalled Humam, who had been the catalyst for his meeting the market people. He admired Humam. His life was a miracle. Humam was a courageous person. A victor! Barman looked at the man huddled in the piece of cloth. *Yes, he wanted even this miserable man to become a victor. He wanted to improve the fates of his friends in the market. Their happiness should not be false or deceptive. Their happiness should be fulfilling.* The horse whinnied. Ssst! He signaled to the horse to be quiet.

Yes, he must wake the man up. He had already wandered around the market. Now it was the time to speak. He had absorbed the magic of the night. He wanted to share a secret. *What had come to Muhammad in the cave?* He wanted to wake the sleeping person and say something to him. The sleeping man would think he was dreaming. How mysterious it would be. Barman would come out of the dark night, unknown and full of secrets. The sleeping man's black pants did not reach his ankles. Surely he was using the sarong to protect himself from the cold. *What are you doing here, sir? Be calm. I come in your dream. My name is Barman. But that name is not important to me now. What's a name for, if in truth we are only a part of something much greater?*

The horse snorted. The sound settled into the night; it was still everywhere. He pressed his hand on the sleeping man's shoulder. Like Barman, he was an elderly man. The man moved. He opened his eyes and blinked at Barman.

Barman was ready to speak. Quickly, he took a deep breath.

"Hey, are you happy?"

The man stirred and looked around. Barman released the man's arm. The old man stretched.

"Mmmmm," he said.

Barman was delighted. "Mmmm" was a satisfying answer. In truth, there would be many people who would answer that question with "mmmm." The man curled up again. *So this was the model of humanity here. Fascinating!* Barman was thrilled. The night felt sacred and magical. He smiled at the moon over the trees.

The round, yellow moon was radiant against the black sky sprinkled with stars. Electric lights illuminated the stillness. The horse's occasional snorts echoed in all directions. A dog barked on and on in the distance. There was a rustling noise from behind the empty drum barrels; it was probably creatures of the night chasing each other. *Serenity is our nature*, thought Barman, *but passion is our life*. He was amazed. *Why had he been so lonely in the middle of the busy city, while here in the middle of nature where it is quiet and sleeping, he was so stimulated and awake?* There was no one around him; everything was still. The old man that he had woken up had already gone back to sleep.

There was someone asleep in a van. An old rickety minibus had stopped at the station. Barman wanted to wake up the person who was sleeping inside. Perhaps he could talk about the person's dreams. Surely the driver was exhausted, had eaten a full meal and then fallen asleep. Someone else was asleep in the back of the van, breathing heavily. Illuminated by the moonlight and the streetlights, Barman could observe these men closely. *Why weren't they sleeping in their homes with their families? Were they happier sleeping out in the open like this?* Barman glanced at the driver inside the minibus. The horse approached the man and nuzzled his ear. The driver stretched. Barman saw his chance to wake him up.

"Hey." He touched the man's shoulder. "Are you happy?"

The man blinked his eyes.

"Mmmm," he replied.

He closed his eyes again, stretched and relaxed.

What an amazing similarity! Were they cut of the same mold?
Barman was determined to wake up everyone who was asleep
around here and ask all of them the same question. He led his horse
down a narrow alley between the market stalls. A breeze carried
a sharp odor towards him: rotting vegetables on the ground. A
dog quietly shuffled away from the bench near a market stall. The
horse flicked his tail when the dog passed near him. Some corners
were completely dark, some spaces were illuminated by moonlight,
while other places were under the streetlights.

Barman found another sleeper. For a moment, when the man
opened his eyes he saw a thin dark shape holding his shoulder.

"Are you happy?"

"Mmmm."

Barman heard honesty in that short reply. It was enough. He led
his horse away. People would wake up and ask each other about his
strange nighttime visit. He stood in the middle of the bus station.
He just stood there stroking his horse, bathing in the moonlight
and breathing the cold night air. He was supremely happy. The
moon, the horse, the tranquility composed the sacred music of the
night. The moon dimmed. From far away came the long, drawn-
out sound of an automobile. A truck entered the station, sounding
its horn. The truck stopped at the station near the market stalls and
the driver's assistant hopped out. He retied his shoelaces. It was still
late at night. Barman watched everything, then he got back up on
his horse and vanished into the darkness.

"Is anyone there?" the truck driver asked.

"Probably not," replied his assistant.

"Wake up, wake up!" the driver shouted.

He sounded the horn again, over and over for a long time. The
old man who was sleeping on the store terrace woke up. He rubbed

his eyes. He was old and wrinkled, but he stood up steadily. The driver's assistant called him. The old man mumbled a reply.

"Is anyone going to the city?"

"Just a moment."

The old man rubbed his eyes again. He started to recall the events of the night.

"Hey, I had a really good dream last night," he said.

The truck driver's assistant studied the old face.

"I'm not asking about your dream. I'm asking about cabbages!"

"Listen. There was a man with a horse. Maybe he was a prince!"

The driver got out of the truck and joined them.

"What did he say?"

"He didn't say anything."

"A man with a horse," the old man continued.

"It was just a dream," said the driver's assistant.

"What dream?" asked the truck driver. "We're here to work, not to get mixed up in anyone's dream."

Other people around the station started to wake up. People in dark clothes stumbled out from the market stalls like sinister creatures emerging from the darkness. They immediately started setting up the stalls. The aisles between the mounds of vegetables began to hum with activity. The truck driver continued to encourage the old man to talk.

"He rode a horse. It was white. He wore a jacket; he was tall and skinny. He woke me up and whispered something… he asked me something."

The old man didn't have a chance to continue when someone approached him and shouted, "Are you happy? Are you happy?"

"That's it! That's it!" said the old man.

The truck driver stared at the newcomer. It was the driver of the minibus who had been sleeping in his van. How could these two men have the same dream?

"We had the same dream!"

"He was tall and thin!"

"Old, skinny!"

"White horse!"

"That's right!"

The driver shouted, "That wasn't a dream! That really happened!"

"Yes, it really happened," said the newcomer. "I was sleeping in my minibus when a horse whinnied outside. It was white in the moonlight. The man asked me, 'Are you happy?'"

"That's so strange!"

"Who was he?"

They were silent. A dim image nudged the old man's consciousness.

"I'm sure that I've seen him before. I'm sure I have!" he said.

"Who was he?"

They stood together bewildered in the early hours of morning. The moon was still shining. There was some activity at some of the stalls, but there were no customers yet.

The truck driver became impatient. This wasn't his concern. He had come to pick up cabbages to take to the city. Some merchants were busy in their stalls. He stepped away from the crowd and shouted, "Hey, who's going to the city?"

The people dispersed, leaving only the old man who remained sitting on the ground. Several vendors headed for the truck to load their vegetables. The vegetables had been piled in their stalls since the previous evening, waiting for the transport from the city in the early morning. In a moment, the bus station was transformed into a bustling terminal. With a roar from the truck, exhaust billowed forth from its pipes and slowly diffused in the haze of the streetlights, the fading moonlight, and the early morning mist. The truck rumbled off into the distance. Those who did not depart for the city with their vegetables returned to catch a few more moments of sleep. Some men smoked. They sat together briefly, then slipped back to their dreams.

When the morning sky reddened, a man who had been sleeping in a market stall went over the man who'd been sleeping on the storefront sidewalk.

"I can't sleep," he said.

"Me too."

"We've seen him before."

"Yes, he's the man who fainted the other day!"

"The one we took home."

"The skinny one."

"The old guy!"

"Who has a white horse!"

"It wasn't a dream!"

"It really happened!"

"What did he say?"

"He said, 'Are you happy?'"

"Ah, we're all miserable!"

"We're not happy!"

Immediately a crowd gathered. Several women carrying loads on their backs placed their merchandise down on the sidewalk under the dimming lights. They placed stools on the ground, sat down, and arranged their goods around them.

The crowd around the old man grew bigger. Their loud voices attracted the attention of other people. Those who had slept in the market stalls came out to hear the news. Usually they quickly crowded around the women food vendors on the sidewalk to buy their breakfasts, but now they were more interested in listening to the old man who was talking about the prince on the white horse.

"He was smiling!"

"He was happy!"

"He's the only one!"

"We're not!"

The old man surveyed the people around him.

"Are all of you happy?"

The people in the crowd looked at each other. They each answered the question privately.

Finally one man replied, "No!"

"We're suffering!"

"We're miserable!"

Laments passed from mouth to mouth. They became a crowd of depressed people, cursing their anxieties. It began with the people gathered at the storefront. The women food vendors joined them as they wondered about their regular customers who were not eating. They whispered. What was happening? Everyone's appetites seemed to have vanished.

"Where does he live?"

"The skinny man who came to us at night."

"I want to meet him!"

"Me too!"

"Is he happy?"

"Yes, he's the only one who's happy!"

"Let's look for him!"

Silence descended on the group. Streaks of sunlight filled the early morning sky. The eastern sky awash with red. Trees tinged with red. The market stalls stained with red. A gentle warmth in the thinning morning mist. The streetlights had been turned off, leaving the poles and lines and lines of black wires.

More people arrived, hurrying along the storefront sidewalk, stopping at the stalls and on the street. The crowd on the storefront sidewalk had not yet dispersed. Several men and women were waiting for a car, and when one approached, they quickly surrounded it. They lived busy hurried lives. But life stopped still on the storefront sidewalk! The people there were deep in conversation.

"How dare he!" shouted a fat man in the crowd.

"Why?"

"That man is terrorizing us!"

"Why?"

"He's making us miserable!"

The crowd erupted around the fat man. The old man who had slept on the storefront sidewalk faced him.

"Shush! Shush!"

"Yes, he's messing everything up!"

"Shush! Shush!"

The old man could not deny that. The fat man screamed out his curses.

Before anyone got angry with him, the fat man declared, "He's making us miserable!"

"How?"

"With that question!"

"That question?"

"That's the source of our misery! Curse him!"

The crowd did not understand him and soon the fat man disappeared. The people soon forgot about him. The old night watchman was more interesting than the fat guy. The people turned away from the shouted curses and towards the soft whispers. But even the whispers started to fade. Several of the men sat down in front of the women food vendors. The anxious crowd formed a circle around the old night watchman.

"Let's look for that man," said someone.

"Yes. We already know where his house is."

"Surely he'll have an answer to that question!"

They still remembered everything. They remembered that day and the man who had fainted. He was thin, old, and had bright eyes. They remembered the entourage to his house and that on the way they met the corpse! They did not understand what had happened at the time, and even now they did not understand!

Then, at the storefront, a decision was made. No one knew who initiated the movement, but the crowd began to move away from the stores and the stalls, and they headed to the street. The people who had seen the old man on the day he had fainted followed the crowd. Several people came out of the food stalls along the way and asked the people in the crowd where they were going. No one answered. The night watchman joined the entourage.

"Why are we going to meet him?" someone asked.

"Are you happy?" said someone else.

"Mmmm."

"Now, come with us!"

The passengers sitting in a bus watched the group as they passed. Everyone still in the market talked about the group that had just left. They ended every conversation about the group by shaking their heads. No one knew why the group had left. The market resumed its usual activities, despite the absence of some of its occupants. The bus started to move and everyone began to drown themselves in their own concerns. The warmth of the sun replaced the morning chill. Patches of sweat started to appear on the shirts of the station coolies. The crowd that had left the market was quickly forgotten, except by the women whose husbands had left them behind.

That morning Poppy woke up as usual. She pulled open the window curtains and caught the sunshine. Wind swept through the pine needles outside the house. As she watched the movement of the pine trees, she noticed someone. *Ah, it looks like old Barman! On his horse, sitting straight and tall. On top of a hillock, facing the sun. What are you doing there, Papa?* The sight made her heart pound. *The power of a miracle!*

Barman was truly a rider. If Poppy still had the right to feel anything, she felt sorry for him. As in a fantasy, the white horse stood bathed in the sunlight with its rider sitting silently, calm and serene, with the sun overhead and a bright sky behind him. Poppy closed her eyes; she hoped that it was only a hallucination. The man sitting on the horse was from the world of shadows. She didn't realize that when she closed her eyes, a few teardrops slipped through her eyelashes. She didn't understand; she didn't want to admit what she was feeling. Whenever she awoke in the morning and she found that her pillow was damp, she didn't want to admit that something was bothering her. She wanted to forget everything except the awareness that she was still alive and happy.

Poppy opened the door and walked towards the image of the rider. *How should she greet old Barman?* She wanted to do what was appropriate; she wanted to express her feelings for him. She could only fulfill the role that had already been determined for her. Her role now was the role of the woman who saw a man sitting on a horse one morning out in the open air. Poppy called him. She saw the horse turn around.

"What are you doing there, Papa?"

That was the normal way to ask him something. From atop his horse, Barman replied. It had been a long time since she had heard his voice.

"Looking at the sunrise, Poppy."

"How long have you been there?"

"All night, I think."

"You didn't sleep all night?"

"No."

"You must be very tired, Papa."

"Look! I'm healthy! Rejuvenated!"

Barman got down from his horse. Poppy invited him into the house. She already knew what she would do. The conversation flowed smoothly.

"You've gotten thinner, Papa."

"Yes, I feel a bit lighter, Poppy."

"You must think more about your health, Papa."

Barman looked at Poppy. "You're still the way you were at the beginning, Poppy."

"Of course."

"Are you happy?"

"Of course, very happy."

"I feel like I'm heading in that direction, Poppy."

Poppy laughed, then she stopped. She really shouldn't have laughed. Barman appeared very old and thin. She was worried about him, but she couldn't do anything about it.

"You're a strange woman, Poppy."

"What do you mean, Papa?"

"How can you be happy?"

Now Poppy really wanted to laugh so that the old man would be sure that she meant what she had said, even though she was aware that perhaps he was laughing at her as well.

Poppy invited Barman into the house. He settled in the guest chair. She closed the door again and quickly headed for the kitchen. She wanted to show Barman the thermoses of warm water and tell him that if he wanted to take a bath, she could prepare it right away. She returned to the living room with the thermoses that she always kept ready.

"You must take a bath with warm water first, Papa."

Before Barman could reply, she added, "Do you want milk or just coffee, Papa? The water will be boiling in just a minute!"

Barman's horse wandered around in the yard. The morning birds twittered cheerfully, and freely circled the house. No one ever bothered them. Nature flourished under the morning sun! As Poppy wiped down Barman's weary body with warm water, he told her that he enjoyed watching the sunrise, but he didn't mind leaving that view if it meant that he would be bathed by Poppy's soft hands. The bath was refreshing after a sleepless night. Barman had to admit that the woman had helped him to stem the effects of ageing. Poppy suggested that Barman take a nap as soon as he had finished breakfast.

His bed in this house was always kept neat and tidy. The sun was high in the sky and Poppy was careful so that Barman was not bothered while he slept. She was surprised to see several people standing outside the house. She was afraid that their voices would wake him up. *Why had they come?* They peered into the house through the windows. Poppy wondered how Barman had gotten involved with those people. Some of them approached the white horse that was grazing in the yard. Then Poppy remembered that these were the people who had brought Barman home the other day.

Poppy tried to be friendly to them, because she had not had the chance to thank them previously. She carefully asked them to speak softly. She said that she could handle any business they had with Barman. The people said that they did not have any business with the old man; they just wanted to see him. They were willing to wait until he woke up.

When Barman opened the door, the people immediately crowded around him. The thin old man was perplexed about their arrival, as they thought he would be. They stared at Barman for a long time without saying anything. After a while, the old night watchman stepped forward.

"We've come, Bapak."

The crowd looked at Barman. He appeared fresh and healthy. The sun outside was bright and blazing. Barman's face was pink, refreshed from his nap. It was quiet. No one spoke until the old night watchmen felt that he should become the spokesman.

"Is it true that you came to us last night?"

Barman nodded.

"What did you really mean?" the night watchman asked.

"We want to ask you something," someone else said.

The crowd shifted. They whispered.

"Yes. What should we be asking?"

"All right," said Barman. "I know what you mean. The answer is: ignorance."

Barman left the house and the people followed him. Poppy watched the group move away from the windows. She closed the door. Her Barman had left with those people! Water was boiling in the kitchen; it was for Barman, but the old man had left. She told herself that her job was over. Unlike the previous times when Barman had left, she felt now that she would never see him again. Perhaps she had been replaced by all those people. She saw Barman sitting on his white horse surrounded by many people. Slowly the horse began to move away. The group of people followed closely behind. She had seen that group come to the house once, but now the entourage was going away, leaving her alone. She sensed that she was about to lose something.

The group quietly left the house and yard. They passed the furthest boundary, a mound of earth. Then she lost sight of them as they disappeared into the green overgrowth. Poppy went to the kitchen. *Just forget that something has happened, Poppy.* She tried to convince herself that everything was all right. She would have to tell Bobby when he asked about his father. *It's like this, Bobby, your father... now....* Ah, she would think of something to say. The son never asked her about anything. The driver who brought the food never brought any messages or orders from him. She knew that Bobby was busy. In fact, she would deceive him if necessary. Now her job was to continue living. She tried to whistle as she returned to the pot of boiling water. Everything was all right. She felt strong enduring her life alone on the mountain, perhaps forever. Perhaps something else would happen to her. She was ready for anything. Whatever happened, it would strengthen her commitment to life. Poppy was sure that life was worth living. *Life is sacred. Poppy is devoted to you, Poppy.* The thought that she had passed judgment upon herself was quickly dismissed. No, she was healthy now, far from ill. She longed to continue living. *Live, Poppy, live.*

6

There were new people around old Barman in the house he inherited from Humam. Poppy faded into a dim memory of his past. There were people everywhere who were interested in watching his every move. Whenever he wanted anything, he just had to ask for it. The people asked him constantly: "What do you want?" But, strangely, he no longer wanted anything. He tried to think of something, but it was useless. He tried to recall what had occurred since his arrival on the mountain and his life in the city. No, he was bewildered. Lying down, sitting and walking under the watchful eyes of these people erased all his thoughts about his own desires. He could have asked them: "What do you want, my children?" But he had never asked them that, because he knew that they would not answer. The house was engulfed in silence. The whole world was encircled in an uncertain silence. In truth, the days were filled with abundance and prosperity, new loyal friends, and overflowing with food. There was no food as fresh as the food of those mountain people!

Fruits freshly picked from the garden were piled high in his room. He liked fruit. But his voracious appetite for food was also silent, as was his mouth, and even his mind. He had become dull and he lost his taste for food to the point where he was worried about his health. His health had been the main consideration for his decision to move to the mountain, but now it was threatened. This could not continue. The abundant food that he had now was different from Poppy's food; it was served straight from nature. *After all, we are in the mountains.* Unfortunately, however, it was not to his liking. He ate a bit of the food only because he was concerned about his health.

He did not know yet whether he liked this new world or not. He was already deep within it, and he accepted this. The people around him, his house, nature, the sun whose warmth he meditated upon daily—all of this had simply come his way and he could not refuse any of it. Would this last forever? Sometimes he yearned for eternity, sometimes he feared it. The only path for him was to accept and live in this new world. There was nothing more than that. He tried to gracefully accept his fate. It was useless to resist it, just as it was useless to hope.

When he thought about Bobby, he sometimes harbored regrets about his son. It was Bobby who brought him to the mountain where all of this had unfolded. If he had remained in the city and lived with his grandchildren, none of this would ever have happened. Ever. If he returned to his grandchildren, he would have to leave Poppy, leave the people around him, and leave the mountain. Would that be possible now? Bobby sometimes passed through his thoughts, very, very distantly. He would soon erase all those memories. So, too, his memories of Poppy, who lived only a short distance away from his new home. *What are you doing now, my Poppy?* He often wondered about her.

Barman had nowhere to return to. He was being dragged along by life. He was well aware of this. The only solution was to accept it peacefully. He once asked one of the people why they were there. "It makes us feel happy, Bapak," the person replied. Amazing! Of course, he could not evict the people who had come voluntarily and did not make a fuss. There was no law or police or rule of etiquette that prevented them from being there. How long would this last?

Ever since it began, Barman had difficulty answering that question. He had no idea when it would end. Let it be. It was better for him to just float on the surface of whatever was happening. This is what he did during the early days. It felt like an unbelievable dream coming true. Dream and reality were interwoven in his mind.

The little house was filled with countless people. Some arrived at night, some arrived in groups; no one disturbed the reverent silence. Many left early in the morning, perhaps to go to the market or to their fields, and they returned at some time during the day. They made the little house their second home. They came to sleep or rest. Even though silence reigned in the house, no one was gloomy or despondent. Several people kept guard at night, either resting, strolling in the nearby fields, smoking, and chatting with each other. Barman tried to take care of himself. Apparently he could live on the mountain without a Poppy to help him.

One night he wanted very much to visit Poppy, the beloved companion he had left behind. He sighed as he thought about her living alone. *Ah, my Poppy. What has happened to you, my sweet one?* Barman called his horse. The people who were sitting in the yard watched him, but they did not say anything. Quietly several of them followed the horse's trail.

Barman circled his old house, imagining Poppy fast asleep in the midst of beautiful dreams. *Be well, Poppy, enjoy your sleep.* He wanted to knock on the door and return to sleep beside the woman. Of course, he would not do that. He felt that he had made an agreement with Poppy. The woman tried not to bother him by taking care of him, and he now would let her sleep peacefully in her room. He stopped the horse at one spot in the garden. He recalled that this was the place where, when they had first arrived, he had rolled on the ground with Poppy, unintentionally pinching her blouse as if the pine needles were still clinging to it. He could no longer return to Poppy.

As he turned to return to his new home, he stopped briefly at the front door. Sitting on the horse, he could see a piece of paper posted on the door. He got off the horse and slowly approached the door. He wanted to open it. A piece of paper was pasted to the glass pane. A message was written with charcoal: "Papa, I'm waiting for you." This was Poppy's handwriting! A simple sentence, beautifully shaped letters. Barman rubbed his old eyes. He touched the glass pane on the door. And he struggled to restrain the feelings that tugged at his heart. *This is your honesty, your purity, your sincerity that I, an old man, cannot bear. Poppy, forgive me.* He stood at the door, trying to calm himself. Tears flowed. *My angel! I can no longer return to you.* Or, perhaps he could return and new, unimagined possibilities would emerge? No, he must accept his present fate.

Slowly, he returned to his horse. He could not erase the written message from his mind; he saw it everywhere—in the black darkness, on the face of the hills and amongst the trees. The horse took him back to the little house. He fell asleep as he rode.

When he neared the little house, he stopped. The sight of firelight disrupted the precious images of his visit to his old house. Torches were on the move everywhere! He could see people carrying torches, pushing their way through the grass as if they were looking for something. They were searching for him! The people who had started to follow him had been left behind because he had ridden off very quickly. Now they were searching for Barman. The moon was dim and almost swallowed in darkness. Barman heard people shouting, "Don't leave us, Bapak!"

Their calls made his heart pound. He did not know these people. Not one of them knew anything about him. One of the torch-bearers approached him. He was surprised when Barman said, "I'm not leaving, son." *I am here. Not in the grass.* Soon other torch-bearers arrived. They stopped their frantic calling and gathered around Barman, relieved. Peace had been restored. The entourage returned to the hut.

Barman asked the fellow who took his horse's lead, "Why were you looking for me, son?"

The man was silent. The others were quiet as well.

"We were worried, Bapak! You were gone!" said someone behind him.

Several people joined them. The ones that had gone down the mountain slope with torches quickly recognized Barman on his horse. The black shadow of the thin man on the horse swept over the hillside. Everyone who joined them shouted, "Bapak!"

Barman stayed on his horse. What was happening? Just at that moment he wanted to return to Poppy; life with her was simple and the restful days were filled with canned food, the flower garden, and the woman's gentle touch! But Poppy was over there in the distance, hidden in the darkness, an untouchable angel behind the clouds, waiting for him. The smoke from the torches, the smell of burning oil, the whispers, the light footsteps of many people, the horse stepping through the grass. Red flames moved on the hillside, darkness lay beyond.

An old man was waiting for the searchers in front of the cottage. He looked directly at the group.

The tension of the moment was shattered by his cry, "Bapak, don't leave us!"

He headed straight for the group. Barman stopped his horse in front of the old man.

The man said plaintively, "We were worried, Bapak!"

He grabbed Barman's foot and would not let go.

"Bapak, don't leave us!"

The crowd watched quietly.

Suddenly several voices rang out together of the crowd, "Bapak, don't leave us!"

People held Barman's foot as if they were afraid that he would leave. The usually tranquil group transformed into a wailing mob.

"Promise us, Bapak!" they pleaded.

Barman waited for the right moment to reply. When they began to calm down, he said heavily, directing his words towards the crowd, but meaning them as a commitment for himself: "Calm down. I will not leave you. My life is your life, your life is my life!"

His voice was clear and everyone could hear him. They breathed a sigh of relief. Then the group began to move again.

The yellow flare of the torches reached the trees, shadows stretched out on the ground, and in the distance, stars twinkled. The chill of the mountain melted, not by the flames, but by their happiness. In the silence, happiness, like the torches, stirred their feet forward. Soon they arrived at his house.

"Don't leave, all right, Bapak?" someone said.

"I'll never leave, son," said Barman.

"We love you, Bapak."

"Our hopes lie with you, Bapak."

"Without you, we are alone."

"We need you."

"We cannot be separated from you ever again."

Barman got off his horse. They helped him down and gently lowered him to the ground.

"Don't leave, Bapak."

"Ever."

"Never, son," said Barman.

"We're afraid."

"We're worried."

Barman stopped the chatter. He stood in front of the house.

"Listen. I will not leave you. I swear!"

They mumbled with relief.

"We're happy!"

"We're so happy!"

"We won't be afraid again!"

The torches were extinguished and the house was engulfed in darkness again. Only a few small lamps were placed in the room, not to provide light to the space, but to light the cigarettes. There were black heaps were scattered about on the floor.

That night Barman realized how much these people needed him. He realized also that he could no longer leave them. He needed these people as much as they needed him. They were different from Poppy. These people were truly dependent on him. The cottage had become a lodging for men. Someone began to tend to the unkempt yard. Someone else brought a hoe and planted mountain flowers. The men who did not go down the mountain during the day entrusted their livelihoods to their wives, and those who did not have wives and did not work ate whatever food the other people brought. Barman's job was just to be there. He saw the newly planted roses begin to bloom and took it as a sign of new friendship that would not be broken. Barman genuinely needed them, but he never asked them to promise to stay with him. This new life was pleasant, like a fascinating strange adventure. *Every day brings something new*, he thought. *Life flourishes!*

The entire market knew about this group. Wives allowed their husbands to go up the mountain. Even without the men, the market was still busy. Those who did not leave their jobs during the day appeared with their wives in the market, guarding their merchandise or bargaining for deals. They did not care about anything other than that; nothing had changed at the market except that the night watchman no longer worked there. Anyone who was willing took a shift in guarding the market at night. There were no disruptions; the children and wives who had been left behind allowed the men to leave, and life went on as usual. The market was lively during the day. The men told their wives that something important was happening. The Bapak was going to reveal a secret! So they diligently left for the cottage every evening, hoping to hear a revelation.

Whenever they arrived at the cottage in the evening, they asked the old watchman what the Bapak had said that day. The old man always shook his head. After the night of Barman's visit to Poppy's house, Barman slipped into silence again. Everything happened on its own—meals, baths, and walks—everything, in total silence.

Several people had brought bamboo tubes to channel water from a spring higher up the mountain, and they now had running water in the back of the house. They took baths, fetched drinking water, and watered the plants. At night they could hear the sound of the crystal clear water flowing. The house was surrounded by fresh grass and blossoming flowers. The new plants began to flourish under the care of these mountain people, who were skilled at tending plants. Barman often strolled amongst the plants, his face glowing radiantly. No longer were dead leaves left lying in the yard. Barman's new friends swept, raked, and gardened enthusiastically. They cut back overgrown grass and built a stall for the horse. Barman noticed all of these changes.

Eventually, everything that needed to be done at the cottage was finished. The men began to sit and lie about again. The old man who always followed Barman around continued to tend to his needs. Even though Barman did not need any help, the old man was always at his side. When it was late at night and Barman had gone to sleep, the men would begin to settle into their own sleeping places in the other room. They were silent or whispered quietly.

"It's almost planting season," said someone.

"And we're not getting anything done here."

"Why are we here anyway?"

"I'm happy here."

"With our Bapak."

"It's peaceful here."

"How long will we be here?"

"Forever."

Barman heard that conversation. He always listened to the men's whispers. He sat on the bed, looking at the floor. Then he lay down and gazed at the ceiling. *When would it end?* He wondered about that as well. He had accepted the situation and tried to feel happy. But of course he knew that it would end at some time. *Why were they here?* He wanted to tell the men outside: asking questions is stupid. *Why must a person ask a question if that question does not pacify his heart? Damn the question!* But Barman did not dare say that to the people who came to him with questions, especially since he had a question of his own. He recalled the night in the market when he had woken some of them up. *Yes, he had poisoned them by giving them the courage to ask a question. Ah, if only he had followed Poppy's advice. That woman was wiser than he was. He should be ashamed. And Humam! His courage was astonishing. No, he did not need to think anymore; he only needed to move, move, move.* He wanted to suggest to the men outside his room to return to the market, to use their muscles, to tire themselves out, and then to fall asleep. *Thinking is our enemy, my sons.* But unfortunately, it was their thinking that had brought them to Barman.

He could not order them to leave. He lived with them in the cottage and he could not leave them. It was best to let time pass. He wanted to see what was going to happen, how the situation would finally end. *What would he do? What would they do?*

Was it Humam or Poppy who had brought him here to this point in his life? He could not blame anyone, especially not the well-intentioned Bobby. Bobby truly understood his father. This life demands that a person comply, if necessary without asking. That was his decision.

Once the old night watchman pestered him, "Tell us, Bapak. Anything! Why aren't we happy?"

Barman almost revealed what he was thinking at that time, but he restrained himself. It was awkward to order people to stop thinking. Meanwhile, the crowd grew bigger. He noticed new people at the cottage.

He had never imagined that many people would come to live there. They trudged up and down the mountain to their houses, the market, or their fields in the chill of the night or the early morning, walking in darkness.

The old watchman begged him more and more often, "Tell us, Bapak. Tell us anything!"

Barman's silence grew deeper and deeper. He saw that their eyes were full of hope, and he almost understood now what they were hoping for. He realized that he had to take responsibility for their coming to the cottage. They had been attracted to him. Sometimes at night he heard them complaining. Their eyes were anxious, searching. He realized that they had placed their hopes in him. What kind of disappointment would befall them?

One night he felt trapped by their presence. Alone in his room, he heard the crowd outside demanding something from him, and he ignored them. When the men were asleep, he carefully opened the bedroom window. How strange it was that he had to sneak out of his own house! It was cold, so he wrapped his jacket tightly around himself. Once he was outside, he could not bear the urge to run away from the cottage. The darkness of the night gave him hope that he would be able to run and hide in the shadows. The darkness of eternity would save him. It would be better than being caged up with people who had expectations of him. He could see the bus station and market in the distance; the streetlights shone dimly through the haze. He could go there, get a taxi, escape to the city, and disappear. Or he could disappear into the darkness anywhere. This would be his revenge upon the people whom he had woken up in the middle of the night in the market. How harsh he was! He found his horse. "Be quiet!" he said to the horse. "We're going on a long journey." He led the horse out of its stall and jumped on its back.

Suddenly he felt someone touching his foot and restraining him.

"Where are you going, Bapak?"

It was the night watchman. *Ah, your old red eyes never stop watching me, grandfather.* Barman realized that he would not be able to escape. Then, suddenly all the inhabitants of the cottage woke up and gathered around him.

"Don't leave us, Bapak!"

"Don't leave us, Bapak!"

The night watchman helped him to get down from the horse. Barman felt at this moment that he was indeed imprisoned. *You have captured me, my children.*

"Without you, Bapak…" several of the men moaned.

Barman stopped listening to them. He returned to his room. Everyone in the cottage stayed awake for the rest of the night.

From a gap in the window shutters Barman knew that sunrise had touched the mountain. When he heard someone unlock the door, Barman realized that the door had been locked from the outside. The night watchman entered.

"I'm sorry, Bapak. But please say something to us. We're afraid. We're miserable. We're worried."

Barman stood up. He was irritated. "We're all haunted," he said.

The people outside the room were silent, but they pushed to enter the room, wanting to hear more.

"Haunted by what?" the night watchman asked.

"Our thoughts!"

The people who were in the room looked at each other. The red sunrise poured through the glass door.

They whispered, "We're haunted by our thoughts!"

The statement passed from mouth to mouth. The crowd transformed into a field of whispers that started out softly and became increasingly louder. Barman left them. He stood apart from them, tense, as if he were watching a mesmerizing performance that was beyond understanding.

Not one person left for work that morning. They formed groups and repeated the words over and over again. Something important had happened. It was the statement from Bapak: "We are haunted by our thoughts!" Barman had given them something extraordinarily important. He knew it was because of these words that they did not go to the market.

He could no longer return to his earlier life. He would move on with his new life and try to identify the more interesting elements of it. *But was this life real or imagined? There didn't seem to be a difference. He could not refuse it. Could he make plans? No! That would be difficult.* He refused to think. He resumed singing after bathing while people conversed near him and talked about him. If he wanted to run, then he occasionally he would run. Everything would carry the same meaning for him. It was a major victory that he could sing in this situation. Poppy, Bobby, and his daughter-in-law, who were now beyond reach, would be pleased to see this development.

The only remaining thing that reminded him of his past was the white horse. But one day the horse disappeared from its stall. As Barman was reminiscing about his wanderings around the mountainside, he realized that the horse was gone. Barman knew that the men had hidden it. He was furious. *You have stolen away my life, now you have taken my horse!* He searched for the old night watchmen.

Incensed, he shouted at him, "What have you done with my horse?"

"It was them! It was them!"

"It was you!"

People gathered around them. Barman glared at them all as they sheepishly lowered their heads. No one dared to look him in the eye.

Timidly, people in the crowd whispered, "We're afraid that you'll leave us."

"Bring it back! Now!"

The crowd quickly dispersed. Barman was left alone for a long time to think about what had just happened. He was furious, frustrated, disgusted, and above all, confused about these overwhelming emotions. He became short of breath. He became dizzy and weak in his joints, then he lost consciousness. He was carried into his room and someone sprinkled rose water over him.

The people were whispering outside his room.

"The horse must be returned."

"But then he'll run away."

"We'll ask him to promise."

"We're getting more confused!"

"More ignorant!"

"My mind is stuck!"

"We're being tortured here."

"We're tortured everywhere."

They returned the horse to the stall and supplied it with fresh grass.

When Barman recovered, he went straight to the stall, and when he saw that the horse had been returned, he hugged it. *My fate is your fate, my horse. You are the one part of my past that is still with me now.* The people saw how much Barman loved the horse and they felt guilty that they had tried to separate them. Barman stroked his horse lovingly. *You are also the only element of nature that has bared its soul to me. Especially in comparison to those people. They are foisting the responsibility of their lives on to me. They are trying to free themselves from the burdens of life and throwing them on me. Why not on the Prophet? Why not on those who voluntarily take responsibility for the behavior of other people?* Barman felt that he had aged. Perhaps his hair had gotten whiter, his body thinner. Why did he ever have to meet these people? He did not understand. When did it start—if indeed there was a beginning to these events? Or were they all suddenly thrown into this situation and no one could avoid it? *It was not that he could not avoid it. He would not avoid it!* He tried to breath spirit into his lackluster eyes. He looked around at the people when he returned from the stall; the sparkle in his eyes had returned.

They greeted him. Someone said, "Say something, Bapak."

This was what that they were asking for.

Gently, Barman greeted them. "Wait!" Then he left them.

He was constantly deliberating about what he should do. *I am not thinking, I am deciding. I am doing. This thinking is a part of the doing.* He had promised them something. Yes, something important will happen. In reality, he was tormented. Yet at the same time, he was pleased because the people in the cottage were in exactly the same situation as he was. They, too, were imprisoned by their fears, both personal and shared. It was a relief to know that he was not alone. There were others in the cottage who had the same fears and questions that he had.

Once Barman awoke in the middle of the night and watched the other men sleeping. He felt compassion for them. Did he love them as well? *We are all suffering, my sons. We are all ignorant of why we are suffering. If you insist that I reveal something to you, then you*

must wait. With any luck we will be able to do something together. No,
we will not be leaving anything behind. We will be entering into it,
but in a better way.

Barman woke up early and refreshed. His wrinkled face glowed
with morning brightness. Around him were the mountain birds,
the dewdrops hanging on the trees, and the warm morning sun.
His eyes sparkled. The inhabitants of the cottage noticed the
difference. Those who were going to go down the mountain to
work that morning whispered, "Our Bapak looks young again."

Barman asked the night watchman to keep everyone from
leaving that morning. He was going to say something important to
them, so they gathered together.

"We are going on a journey," Barman announced to the
group. "Our journey will be as important as any journey in all
human history. The journey of the prophets, the wise men, the
philosophers."

They listened carefully. They looked around at each other.

"Where are we going, Bapak?"

"To the top of the mountain. There!" Barman pointed to the
distant mountain peak.

"We are going on a hike, so get ready!"

"When?"

"Tomorrow morning. Only those who want an answer may
come."

Everything was astir. Tomorrow morning! An important
journey! They looked up to the mist-covered mountain peak. Many
of them had been up the mountain before, and even though the
mountain peak had always stirred strong feelings in them, the trek
up the mountain had never been an important event. For those
who were born on the mountain, the peak symbolized the highest
and most excellent of achievements. Young people liked to climb

it for adventure; older ones felt that the chill of the mountain air brought clarity and tranquility. Now they would be traveling there with the old man, the bearer of their hopes.

Barman was pleased with this decision. He had finally dared to take a step. He was wildly happy. They were going to the mountaintop! Was he going to say something? Or do something? Yes, he was ecstatic. There was warmth in his chest the entire day; he was quivering with excitement. A strange, very secretive, unfamiliar world was going to be revealed. He sensed that something significant was going to happen to all of them, and it moved him deeply. *We are going to enter a strange, magnificent, and magical world. Poppy and Humam and anyone who doesn't come with us will not experience it.* He wanted it to be a special experience, just for those on this journey. He was prepared to pay for it with his life. Was he? Really? *Keep moving. Don't stop in the middle of the road. You cannot determine the direction. Everything will move on its own. You are in the middle of it. It is best that you just follow along with whatever happens.*

That day the house was quiet. The men went down the mountain to the market or to their fields to inform their wives of the journey. Only the old night watchman stayed in the cottage. He just sat there all day. His eyes did not leave the distant mountain peak—the mountain peak was covered in mist, as life had veiled his aged eyes.

Barman prepared himself for a possible separation from Poppy, Bobby, Dosy, and his grandchildren. He would soon leave Humam's cottage. He looked into the distance below, in the direction where his son lived. *I can no longer go there. I can no longer return to you. This journey has taken me too far away, son. I ask nothing of you.* Let them think whatever they wanted to think. The mountain peak! That was a new place! And what would happen there? *Ah, why think about it now, before anything happens?* When the moment comes, there will be other things to think about. His decision was based not on thought, but on action. He was going to do something on that mountain peak, at that moment, in that place, in that situation.

That day Barman did not rest. He wanted to observe the seconds pass. It was a kind of farewell to an old friend. Everything was fascinating if you knew that you would never see it again. The sun moved over the pine trees, the clouds, the earth, the waterfall, and the bamboo water troughs that the men had constructed. The horse stall, the house and, yes, it was there that Humam lay at the end of his life. His desire to see his Poppy was satisfied just by gazing in the direction of his old house. His thoughts traced the rose vines, a glimpse of Poppy's dress, a shared meal, and hearing his beloved offering him wine. *"You must be cold, Papa."* He drew a quick breath. *Such a graceful woman; an angel of shimmering moonlight.* Drenched in sweat, he withdrew. That was the house that Bobby had arranged for him. He took shelter under the trees.

The dry pine needles covering the grass reminded him of Poppy. They had once lain down on the grass under the pine trees. *What flowers are you planting now, Poppy? Purple flowers are lovely to see. Have you telephoned Bobby to ask him to send food? What did he ask you? Is your skin will white and glistening? I want to take you by your hand, my love. You should ask Bobby to send turf grass. It's pretty; the yard should be planted with it. I remember that grass at one of the embassies; I forget which one it was. Do you remember me? You haven't changed, have you? I know why you did not come to me. Do you know why I did not come to you, Poppy? I admire your courage. Living alone on the top of the mountain! In your youth! I'm not able to add to or take anything away from the way you live your life, Poppy.*

The old night watchman reminded him to rest. Barman was irritated. *Why did you interrupt my memories?* He had his rights. At the very least, he could still savor his memories.

"What are we going to do tomorrow morning, Bapak?"

"Go on a journey!"

"What for?"

"Isn't a journey something to do, not something for something else?

"Promise, Bapak."

"Promise!"

"I do not want to suffer any more."

"You will be happy, old man."

The old guard's eyes widened. He stood straight. His eyes sparkled with hope.

"Believe me," said Barman. "Something will happen to us. Something that has never happened before, even in our dreams. It will be amazing and unexpected; the miracle of life. It will answer every question you have ever asked."

As the old watchman reflected upon on these words, Barman continued softly, as if speaking only to himself, "And perhaps also another major question."

7

Early in the morning the people were ready for the journey. They awoke soon after sunrise and crowded near the water spout. Some had not slept that night, wondering about the journey they were about to undertake. That morning, the cottage was livelier than usual. More people, men and women, arrived from their homes. Most of them were from the market. The women sat beneath the tree, waiting for the sun to rise higher, covering themselves with their shawls. They had left their homes very early in the morning. The white horse was grazing in the yard. Some of the newcomers admired the horse. Someone had brushed its white coat.

"It's white," a woman said.

"Very white," said another.

"And shiny."

"And tall."

"It's pretty."

"It can run fast."

"As if it's flying, they say."

"No one can run as fast as that horse. It outran everyone once before."

"Is it Bapak's favorite horse?"

"Of course it is."

When the horse approached them, someone pulled up some grass and tossed it to the horse. The horse's tongue extended out to reach the grass. A bright whiteness spread through the pink hues of the early morning sky. The women were pleased; the day had begun brightly and the journey would soon begin.

"You're not selling today?"

"No."

"Who's watching your goods?"

The woman shook her head. "I'm not selling today," she said.

"Me too."

"The market is deserted."

"I thought so."

"We want to join the trip."

They looked at the cottage. Was the trip going to start soon? Inside the cottage everything was proceeding calmly. They saw that the cottage was something other than the busy marketplace where things were bought and sold. The night watchman issued the orders to everyone else. "In a little while," he told anyone who asked. The wait seemed so long!

The sun warmed the hills and freed the trees from the mist. Occasionally they gazed up at the peak. The journey would take all day; they would pass ravines, hills, and forests. The night watchman ordered someone to bring the horse to the cottage. Several men caught the horse and put on its bridle and saddle. Those who were not doing anything asked if it was already time to leave. They gathered around the door, waiting for news about the departure.

They were relieved when the old night watchman stood in front of the door and shouted, "We'll leave soon!"

The horse's groom pushed the other people aside and led the white horse to the door of the cottage. Everyone knew the groom; it was the market groundskeeper. The horse glistened in the light of the morning sun. It stood tall and beautiful. The women repeated their praise. They all waited with hearts pounding.

Barman emerged from his room. The people saw a thin man, tall, with white hair escaping from under his black velvet *peci* cap.

He wore a black jacket and boots. Barman was prepared to climb the mountain. His face was fair and his eyes sparkled beneath his white eyebrows. Barman smiled at the crowd of people. He jumped lightly onto the saddle. The people stared at Barman in awe as he sat on his horse like a statue in a fairy tale. The crowd was silent. When the horse began to move forward, the group started to follow it.

The cottage was quickly deserted. Traces of humanity were left everywhere. They left the dirt, grass, rooms, water spout, and yard. Birds began to chirp again on the rooftop and pick at the pine needles on the ground. After the people left, the animals reclaimed the cottage and began to sing again.

The group passed the residential area of the mountainside. Their hearts throbbed with excitement. Higher up on the mountain, they looked down on the market and the houses below. They felt as if they were leaving something behind, but they did not regret it. Ah, the peak of the mountain! A cluster of clouds covered the peak. They prepared to face the cold mountain air. Several people carried heavy packs. The night watchman had packed necessities for the night, including torches and warm clothing.

Many of the travelers knew the path to the peak. Barman rode his horse slowly so that the older men and women could follow him easily. To clear the path, those in the front slashed back the vegetation along the side of the path. They passed through tall grass and arrived at a pine forest. They could hear the sound of loggers working in the forest. A man carrying an axe emerged from the underbrush and watched the group as they traveled the darkened path through the pine trees and dense forest. Part of the forest was being cleared. All the workers were busy except for the one with the axe.

"What group is this?" he asked one of the crowd.

The reply was just a glance that implied that his question disturbed the travelers. The questioner decided to follow the group.

He sensed the sanctity of the journey.

"Is this a funeral procession?" he ventured to ask again. There was no reply. He continued to follow the group as he counted the heads of the hikers. There were more than thirty people. *Where were they going?* He felt compelled him to keep following them.

There were many other workers in the pine forest. Some of the pine trees were being tapped for the resin. The tappers turned to watch the group. They noticed their friend in the group.

"What group is this?"

There was no reply. They saw a man on a white horse. The workers left the trees and followed the crowd. At first the tappers tried to ask the travelers for an explanation, but it was useless. They all shrugged their shoulders. As if by an unstated agreement, the journey was conducted in silence. Carrying their hoes and axes, the forest workers walked behind the group. They walked easily, but they did not know why they were following this strange procession. The line of travelers stretched out under the trees along a difficult path. Overhanging branches scratched their shoulders. Several times Barman had to push aside branches that blocked his way. The tappers who had joined the group no longer asked questions. Why should they ask? They had felt an urge to join. No one prevented them from following; that was enough. The shade of the trees protected them from the sun. The forest air was cool and gentle.

At the edge of the forest, cold mountain water flowed in a stream. Many members of the group washed their feet in the stream, and Barman's horse drank. Some people filled thermoses with the cold mountain water before continuing on the journey. The mountain people walked as nimbly as the horse. They all walked silently, secretly. Under the trees in the middle of the forest, they were not aware of the sun. Although the sun was now high, it was cool in the mountain forest. They continued on. One by one the forests were conquered, the hills were traversed, the ravines were crossed.

There was no thought of rest. Sometimes the mist concealed their path, but the sun soon emerged to help them. If the path was steep, they slowed down to a crawl. The paths along the edges of the ravines meant death to the careless traveler. The mountain people would not surrender. The mountain peak lay ahead of them. The peak, the horse, the old rider, the secret; they were captivated.

They could do nothing other than conquer the mountain. They were not tired; how could they feel tired if their journey was a dream? It seemed as if the mountain was almost within their reach. They desperately wanted to reach the peak quickly. No, don't stop. The cold mountain air pierced their bodies. They pulled their thick clothes more tightly around themselves.

And now here at last was the peak!

The old night watchman said, "This is the peak, Bapak."

Barman nodded. The white horse stopped.

Raised hands signaled the group to stop. Their feet were freezing. The earth was damp. They stopped. *We've made it!* They looked out over the vast expansive plains. Many of them had been there before, but that day felt different. That day's journey had some extraordinary meaning. They felt as if they could reach up and touch the sky. The mist wound around them, gently playing with their sense of perspective. The sun was still bright, but they felt sheltered. As the sun lowered in the sky, its heat lessened.

Barman sat tall on the horse, watching the sun as it began to fade.

The people sat on the ground wherever they could find a clear space. The women sat together, chattering away while keeping an eye the man on the horse. From their seats on the ground, they looked up at Bapak on the horse, clouds at his back, the mist, the blue sky. It was an unforgettable image. The horse and its rider were rooted at the peak of the mountain and sheltered by the sky, as if they were creatures from beyond the realm of everyday life.

The old night watchman looked around at his friends. He did not expect that the group would be as big as this. Although his vision was blurred by advanced age and the thin mist, he tried to count them, but his effort was useless. He wiped his eyes several times. They were red and heavy.

"We'll stop here, friends," he said.

They lay back or massaged their feet. The packages of food remained untouched. They were hungry, but no one dared to eat. A man approached the night watchman.

"Will we be getting an explanation soon?"

"Explanation?" the watchman replied in surprise. He shrugged his shoulders.

"Bapak promised."

"Promised what?"

"Everything."

Other people approached him, saying, "I don't want to suffer any longer."

A crowd gathered.

"We want to be free from suffering."

"We want to be happy."

"For all eternity."

"No more suffering!"

"Quickly, tell Bapak to end this suffering."

The forest worker with the axe entered the circle.

He asked one of the people, "What are you suffering from?"

The person shrugged his shoulders. At almost the same time, another person also shrugged his shoulders.

The night watchman explained, "We're not happy. That's suffering. We're surrounded by suffering. It imprisons us; it blinds us."

Everyone seemed to agree with his explanation.

They urged him, "Quickly, tell Bapak to put an end to our suffering."

They dispersed and returned to where they had been sitting. But they did not stop watching the white horse.

The night watchman returned to Barman.

"Rest, Bapak," he said. "The horse, too."

But Barman paid no attention to him. He remained sitting tall on the horse. The horse kept flicking its tongue. The night watchman signaled to someone, then several handfuls of grass were offered to the horse.

"Come down here, Bapak," he said to Barman. "Let the horse eat."

The horse stamped its feet, but Barman remained on the horse.

He was alone, the center of attention. One point on the face of the earth beneath the vast sky. The arch of the open sky, hovering over the face of the earth. There sat Barman on his white horse, tall, supporting the sky. There was cold sweat on his forehead. The men and women surrounding him gazed up at him. The sun was fading, glowing red in the sky. They knew that it would soon be evening on the mountain peak. They were worried: soon it would be dark. And very cold. The people began to whisper.

The whispers grew louder and then there was a shout, "Quickly, it's getting late!"

"Yes, it's getting dark!"

The old night watchman looked in the direction of the voices. He knew they were urging him to do something. But what should he do? Barman was still sitting on his horse. The horse pawed at the ground. There was froth dripping from its mouth. The horse was tired. It trampled the grass beneath its feet.

"Bapak," said the old watchman to Barman. "They're asking you to do something soon."

Barman looked at him. The gaze of the two men met.

Barman asked him softly, "What do you want from me?"

The night watchman was quiet. Barman repeated his question. There was no reply.

"What do they want from me? Ask them!"

The loyal old man was flustered. In that instant, he knew that there was nothing more that he wanted, or rather that he wanted something but did not know what it was. He searched for an answer amongst the people in the crowd.

The night watchman shouted, "Hey! What do you want?"

His voice was hoarse. It had begun to darken on the mountaintop; the desolate redness of the sky settled onto the earth. The old man's voice rang out clearly in the wind. The crowd stood up.

"We want to be happy!"

"Show us the way!"

The night watchman looked back and forth from Barman to the crowd.

"We will begin our journey," said Barman.

"We will begin our journey again!" said the old watchman to the people.

They were silent; they looked at each other. Weren't they already at the mountain peak?

"Where else are we going?"

"Where else, Bapak?"

"We can't stand it any longer, Bapak!"

The market groundskeeper and the old night watchman held Barman's horse. They prepared to continue the journey, but not one other person moved.

"Come on!" said the old man.

No one moved. The red sky was unyielding. They had seen the ravine, the hills, the trees reddening in the distance.

"We'll stay here," said someone.

"Until there is no more suffering."

"Until our worries are obliterated."

They were clearly not going to move any further. The old night watchman realized this and asked Barman to say something.

Barman turned pale on top of the horse. The chill on the peak sharpened. The people around him had transformed into an alienating crowd. He felt alone. They made him feel isolated. He was bewildered. *Why was he here? These people! They threw the responsibility for their lives on him. They were his torturers!* He felt trapped. He remembered Poppy. He remembered Humam. He remembered his life in a flash. If he was forced to say something to these people, there was so much he could say. He could even talk to himself if he wanted, but there was no longer any use for words. Words had become his enemies.

Barman shivered. The night watchman said that the evening mist was thickening. The people in the crowd began to worry. They knew that the mist would hinder their journey.

"Come on, let's go home!" shouted the night watchman.

"No!"

"We can't!"

"We haven't gotten anything!"

"We can't go home empty-handed."

"We've been patient long enough!"

The crowd became disorderly. Barman surveyed them. They refused to be quiet.

"What do you want?" the old watchman shouted.

Suddenly they stopped. The old man repeated his question.

"What do you really want?"

"Whatever will make us happy."

"What?"

The night watchman stared.

There were whispers.

"What are we asking for?"

Someone shouted out as if speaking off the top of his head, "We don't know. That's the problem!"

"If we knew, then this would be a waste of time!"

"What don't you know?" asked someone else from another direction.

Others followed the voices, looking back and forth at the ones who were speaking.

"That's what we don't know!"

"What's going on?"

The mist touched the back of the mountain. The chill penetrated the crowd. Several hisses were heard and the voices quickly quieted down.

"We will soon be surrounded by mist," said a voice cracking the silence.

"It will be incredibly cold!"

"We're waiting, Bapak!"

Whispers passed through the crowd; whispers about the mist, about the night that was fast approaching, about Bapak sitting on the horse. The people drew closer to Barman, as if they were afraid of being separated from him. Perhaps the mist enticed them to draw closer to each other. The sun sent out the faintest tips of redness to the farthest corners of the earth.

The night watchman held tightly on to the white horse. The creature was restless. Watching the horse carefully, the old man had a premonition that something disastrous was about to happen. *This is not a mountain horse*, he thought.

The people could not remain silent. As they began to be enveloped in the mist, no one could understand what anyone else was saying. They were restless.

From the midst of the desperate appeals, Barman heard people calling him, "Bapak! Bapak!"

The wings of the mist spread out to encompass the entire peak, thick grayish white mixing with the darkening maroon of the evening sky.

Voices called out, "We're waiting, Bapak!"

And then it was dark. One by one, the voices were silenced by the mist. They stood up and clustered together for warmth. They worried that they would stumble and fall, so they huddled together in the middle of the clearing. Their breathing was short, heavy, cold, and damp. They dared to look only at those closest to them.

Sitting astride his horse, Barman knew that although the people were quiet, their voices were caught in their throats. They were still demanding something from him. He could still see them, whining, moaning, urging, threatening. He did not know what to say. He did not know whether he felt sorry for them or afraid of them or whether he hated them. They were silent in the mist. Barman realized that the mist had clarified something that could not be explained with words. The mist, the mountain peak, the darkness, the crowd, the restlessness. Barman shivered, moved by his feelings, by the mist and the cold mountain peak. He felt something seizing him. But what was it?

"I will speak," he said to the old watchman at his side.

Barman was surprised by his own decision. *What was he going to say?* This was the only way he could free himself from their clutches. Or to enter deeper into it. It would be the same thing. He steadied himself, sitting astride his horse. Warmth spread throughout his body. He felt strong and healthy.

"Our Bapak is going to speak!" announced the night watchman loudly.

In the dark and the mist, the people stood close together. There was only the darkness of twilight and the murmur of their voices. Soon they quieted again. They directed their ears toward the horse and rider, as they could not see Barman clearly in the dark. They just listened for his voice. The mountain peak was like a grave that had appeared suddenly as a place to take a stance.

"He hasn't said anything yet," said someone.

"I hope it's not that we can't hear."

"We're waiting, Bapak!"

"Calm down," said the old watchman.

Barman watched as the people drew closer. They were his friends, his children, his admirers, his devotees, and his judges. They now were hoping, begging, waiting, and also threatening. He asked himself: *Why did he have to stand here and say something? Was he someone named Buddha, or Jesus, or Muhammad?* Then, to his own surprise, he smiled. He felt strong, energized and ready to address the crowd. He was sure that his sentences would flow smoothly and that everything on the mountain peak—the people, the hills, the ground, the mist, and the trees—would hear him and welcome his message. His eyes widened and, as if the mist had dissipated, he saw the people around him clearly.

"This is my sermon," he said.

The wind whipped around people's clothes, through the trees and the grass. Otherwise, there was no movement. The peak was clear. Feet were still. Mouths were closed. And the white horse stood steady, carrying Barman. Barman could hear his voice reflecting off the trees. How clear it was! He continued to speak.

"It is useless to go on with this life!" he screamed.

It was the scream of a hoarse, wounded old man. The people were stunned. Astonished, they repeated what they had just heard. *This life is worthless!* Everyone was quiet, like the mist. They were dumbstruck. The whispers stopped. They were all waiting for something to happen.

"Kill yourselves!" shouted Barman.

Kill yourself! They repeated this command amongst themselves. The mist thickened again and they forgot where they were. Only the fact that they still felt the ground beneath their feet made them conscious that they were still on the earth. Reality seemed so far away; it had become something strange and foreign. Had they

really heard those words? It seemed as if they had lost their sense of
self. They felt empty and hollow. Their legs buckled beneath them.
No one could stand any longer; they all crumpled to the ground.
Where were they now? They felt the earth beneath them, and the
cold. And here, they hesitantly touched their bodies. They felt their
muscles and bones. But they were freezing.

There was a voice, a hoarse cry! Barman's cry.

Some people started to sob. They were weeping together.
Barman's cry, the people's cries. The night watchman began to
strike his chest.

"We're miserable, Bapak!" he said.

The other people began to pummel their chests. The sound of
the pounding, the shouts and the cries filled the mountain peak.
The voices were surrounded by darkness.

"We're in agony!"

Mist moved in upon them as they wailed. There on the peak,
the screams and moans of the men and women echoed in the night,
whipped by the frigid mountain wind.

Suddenly they stopped. The mist was brushed aside by a gust of
wind and dim forms took shape. There was a terrified whinny. It
seemed as if the horse was flying. And then there was the sound of
something tumbling to the bottom of the ravine. Everyone stood
up, petrified. They rubbed their stinging eyes.

The night watchman shouted, "Bapak! Where are you, Bapak?"

They realized that Barman and his horse were no longer there.
Then they recalled the image of flying white horse. The mist came
swirling back.

They shouted, "Don't leave us, Bapak!"

They looked around, but could not see anything in the mist.
"Don't leave us, Bapak!" The voices reverberated down the
mountainside. Chaos broke out on the mountain peak. They were
terrified. They hoped that it was only a bad dream. *No*, they began

to moan. They were on an island of mist, far removed from rest of the world. Where had their journey taken them? They stamped their feet on the ground. Several people began to tear at their clothes. Long heartrending howls came from the men and women in the darkness and mist on the desolate mountaintop.

They could see the final line of red in the west. The mist thinned. Everyone stopped. They looked around. *What just happened?* They were silent.

"Bapak has left us, friends," said someone.

"Our hopes are gone."

"No more."

"We're alone, alone."

"We've been cast aside."

"Left in the darkness."

"We don't know, where should we go?"

"We're lost!"

"We're alone!"

They shouted to each other.

"Our lives are fruitless!"

"Meaningless!"

"Useless!"

"Empty."

"Eternal emptiness!"

The market groundskeeper who had led Barman's horse rubbed his hands together. Had he let the horse escape?

The red in the sky deepened and dissolved, and the peak was swallowed in darkness. They were hoarse from crying. Some sat in stunned silence. The women straightened their veils and wrapped their clothes against the cold.

Then, in the east, a new light was rising—the moon! A full moon about to journey across the night sky. They all looked to the east. The moon!

"The moon is rising!"

"Full moon!"

"Let's go down!"

They began to pack up their things. They wanted to descend the mountain quickly. Traveling in the dark would make their journey difficult.

"Don't rush!" shouted the night watchman. "We have torches!" The people looked at him.

The old man continued, "Why are we leaving our Bapak?"

"Let's look for him!"

The moon provided enough light to illuminate the area around the peak. Only the western part was in shadows. They could see the outlines of everything—boulders, trees, the ground. And they peered down into the ravine beside them.

Someone shouted, "There's something white down there!"

They looked down to where he was pointing. Yes, there was something white.

"It's the horse."

"Yes!"

"Let's go down!"

They peered into the ravine.

"The horse is not moving."

"It's dead."

"And our Bapak?"

They knew the answer, but no one said anything.

Several men descended into the ravine. They pushed aside the shrubs. Soon they were lost beneath dark trees. The moon shone above. More men lighted more torches and followed the search group.

"We'll wait for them here," said those who were left behind.

The people sat down again. They reflected upon the moon and the misty peak. Bright moonlight beamed down into the spaces between the trees. They remembered that it was the middle of the month. They could see the twinkling of electric lights in the distance. The houses and the market far, far below. They waited for the group that had descended into the ravine.

The old night watchman sat on a boulder. He did not move in the dim moonlight. He gazed, unblinking, into the mist. He did not feel the cold that struck his back. The market groundskeeper who had become the horse's groom was also silent. These two men who had been the closest to Barman kept to themselves, reflecting upon what had just happened. No one paid any attention to them.

The torches moved between the trees. Those at the peak knew that the group was returning. Lights were visible briefly and then were swallowed up again in the darkness. Sometimes the lights illuminated distant trees, and a line of yellow lights linked to the moon, sweeping through the blackened leaves. Those who were waiting at the peak watched closely as the group climbed slowly back up the side of the ravine.

They finally reached the top. Those who stood at the edge welcomed them, holding their breath. The torches lighted their way. Several men were carrying Barman's body. They examined it. There was silence on the peak; it was preparing itself to receive the corpse.

"Shall we take him down the mountain?"

The night watchman emerged.

"No," he said.

"What about his family?"

"We are his family. All of humanity is his family." The night watchman continued, "He surrendered himself to us to bury him. Get everything ready!"

The pine forest workers who had brought their hoes offered them to the others in the group. The earth on the mountain peak was rocky, but the mountain men quickly dug a grave. Torches surrounded the diggers. Everyone else gathered around them. Barman's body was laid on the ground, and the women covered it with their scarves. Skillful hands tossed the earth up from the bottom of the pit. They did not find it difficult to dig the grave. Torches lit the sky. The peak appeared to be on fire. Gusts of wind blew on the flames.

They dug a wide grave. The men who were at the bottom of the pit climbed out, helped by the men around the edge. Standing next to each other around the pit, with torches in their hands, they gazed at the grave. Clumps of earth lined the edges of the pit; some dirt crumbled back down to the bottom of the grave as people shuffled along the edge. The old night watchman gave the order to bring the corpse to the grave. Several men carried the corpse. The women turned their faces away because they were afraid to see something terrifying. Barman's face was turned upward to the sky. Someone covered it with a scarf. In the light of the torches, they caught a brief glimpse of the face, pale with white hair, thin, and pained. Lit by the torches, Barman was laid down in the grave. Everyone stood speechless at the graveside. Silence reigned. No one dared to start filling in the grave again. They remained standing near the grave, reflecting upon the body for a long time.

Then gradually, the dirt piled up along the side of the grave began to slide in. The face and body of the corpse was covered with earth. The hoes went back into action and soon the grave was filled. Then all the men and women wanted to pour a handful of earth on the grave. Hands, feet, and hoes worked together. A mound took shape in front of the crowd. They kept looking at it while imagining a creature beneath the earth, moaning.

Black smoke curled upward from the tips of the torch flames. Beads of sweat froze on the men's backs. There was the smell of oil. The moon shone above. No one moved. The old night watchman was still contemplating the mound.

"Friends," the watchman said. "We have buried our Bapak. Look, our hands are still dirty. This earth is holy; don't wash your hands. Here we have buried our friend, our Bapak, our savior. He has taught us something. And, he has become his own first student. He has become the primary actor of his thoughts. He has become the first person he saved. He has freed himself and he is the first who has attained freedom. Remember what he taught us! Long live Bapak!"

He stopped. The people looked at him. They did not move.

Then he continued, "Do not be sad. If you are restless, look at this mountain peak wrapped in mist. Look at the moon. Bapak is up there now. Living in eternal shelter!"

He was out of breath. He had spoken loudly. From the edge of the grave, he pointed to the mound.

"The one who is buried here is the Victor! Victory!"

Then the night watchman began to walk away and the group followed him. One by one they re-entered the forest. Soon they were swallowed in darkness. Under the light of the moon and holding torches, they descended the mountain. The peak was deserted once again. Once again, it was covered by mist. The moon shuddered, desolate.

8

"Don't tell me anything," said Poppy, when she opened the door. It was after midnight. People had gathered outside. The torches had been extinguished. Black shadows were visible in the moonlight under the blackened trees. Stars peeked out from behind the clouds in the sky.

The people had gathered there to tell her about Barman's death. She closed the door quickly, leaving them standing outside lost in their thoughts. They did not understand why she did that. She was the only member of Barman's family that they knew.

"I already know everything," said Poppy from inside the house.

Moonlight streamed into the rooms. Although they were weary, some of the people imagined the beautiful woman in the moonlight. The lights in the house were quickly turned off and the house was left in darkness beneath a gentle moon.

Even though the woman had closed the door, the night watchman went to the window and said, "Our condolences, miss." But Poppy did not hear him. The night wind swept their voices away. The wind rustled through the pine trees in the distance. The people sat down. It was very late at night and their feet were sore. They lay down in the yard. Some of them may have had nightmares about death or beautiful dreams about the woman inside the house. No one understood what had happened that day and night. They were exhausted and sleepy. Mist hugged the trees.

They wrapped themselves in long scarves, sarongs, and whatever they had. No one stirred. They had all collapsed. Even among the trees, there were only dark shadows in the dim moonlight. The old watchman was still standing restlessly in front of the door. From the sounds of the land, it seemed that everyone except the night watchman had fallen asleep. They put down their burdens, lay back and tried to forget that something had happened. Sleep, an element of the beauty of death.

Wearing her thick jacket, the woman who had opened the door to the crowd that night opened it again and left the house. The people sleeping in the yard did not see her carefully threading her way around them. Bathed in the moonlight, she stepped lightly between the sleeping bodies. The house was quiet; the electricity had been turned off. She walked on the damp grass. In just a few steps her shoes were soaked. She walked down the mountain slope towards the dim streetlights at the bus station and the market. The night watchman watched her silently, mesmerized. Was this a dream?

As usual, the bus station was dimly lit. The neon lights struggled to cut through the haze. A dog was sprawled out on the street. The smell of oil oozed out of large barrel drums. There was a trash heap in the corner of the station. Cabbages were piled in the market stalls. People slept soundly, wrapped up in their blankets. Everyone was asleep; there wasn't a single person awake. A dog barked in the distance. The dog that had been asleep on the street suddenly woke up and wagged its tail. It stood up, barked, and staggered away.

There were vehicles parked on the side of the road. Poppy approached them. She wanted to leave this place. When she looked in one car, she could see someone asleep inside. She saw a man who was wearing a nylon shirt on the cold night. A strong body sleeping proudly. A man! She had to leave now! Poppy shivered; an alarming warmth assaulted her. It was a wound that wanted to be avenged.

She stood at the door of the cab, hesitant to open it. Her blood thundered and raced to the lower regions of her body. She stretched and tried to calm herself. Her heart was pounding. She longed to open the door, but she held back. Then, in a quick movement, she opened the door and jumped into the car. Startled, the man inside woke up, blinked at her, and inhaled her enticing fragrance as she dropped herself on to him. She remembered that she had done this before in her previous life; she knew exactly what she had to do. The man's eyes glazed over. Poppy knew better than anyone what she had to do.

She whispered to him as she held her breath, "Be quiet. I'm a woman."

The man stirred. Perhaps this was a dream, but warmth filled his body and he could not resist her. This was reality encased in a dream. It was no longer cold inside the car. It rocked gently. Poppy summoned up all her stored energy; the female volcano erupted. She released her burdens one by one until they were exhausted. They lay side by side. The moon and the streetlights poured over the top of the car's roof, dimly, gently filtering into the interior.

They slept only briefly. When they woke up, chilled by the night, they looked at each other. They remembered what had just happened. Poppy smiled at the man and, hesitantly, the man returned her smile. He wondered how a woman as beautiful as this had been sent from heaven to sleep with him. He gazed at her for a long time. Suddenly, she realized where she was and what she had done.

The man asked, "Just a moment, who are you?"

Poppy opened her eyes wide. The man gazed into her clear eyes. "Does it matter who I am?"

That was enough for the man. Poppy stroked his face. Her touch was so gentle.

"Promise me," begged Poppy.

"What?"

"Take me away."

"Hmm?"

Time was generous to them. Except for the two people inside
the car, the rest of the market was still asleep. The driver and Poppy
spent the night with their dreams. It was cold everywhere else—
in the houses and the food stands, the roofs of the market stalls,
stores, barrel drums, the street, electric lines. A dog sniffed through
the trash.

The people who had surrounded Poppy's house woke up when
the sunrise touched their eyes. They sat up or leaned against the
trees, then looked over at the house. Several men peered inside.
Where was the pretty woman? They had not yet told her about the
death. The night watchman was quiet, still waiting near the door.

"There's no sound," said someone.

"Did she leave?"

They got up and knocked on the door. It was open. They pushed
into the house and searched the rooms, under the bed, even under
the mattress. They finally stopped. No one was there.

"We've lost her."

"There is no other family."

"No one else."

The people searched in the yard, the flower garden, even the tall
grass. When they returned, they shrugged their shoulders. She was
not there.

They packed up their things—packets of spoiled food, the
remnants of the torches, bamboo, and dried grass. Then they
left. They went back down the mountain and left the house
without saying a word. Had they learned something important?
Or something meaningless? They stepped lightly. Was it because
they were filled with new hopes or because they had released their
burdens? Or did they actually not have any burdens? Some of them
sang with the birds that flew by; some of them let their heads hang

down, sweaty and dejected. Some of them whistled and knew that they were still alive even after what they had experienced the previous night. It was only a part of their lives.

"We're lucky."

"There is no longer any hope!"

"There is no longer any desperation!"

"There is no longer any happiness!"

"There is no longer any sorrow!"

"And we are left with our lives!"

"That are perfect!"

"That are empty!"

"This is deliverance!"

"We have experienced perfection!"

"It's the same for all of us!"

"There's no longer any conflict!"

"Our lives, our lives are the only things that are absolute!"

"Long may we live!"

They descended the mountain slope and headed for the market. The people would gather together there. They would separate, then gather again. They let their feet lead them. They would greet each other and fall silent again. The sounds of morning surrounded them; their steps were soft on the grass. The sun overhead, red, warm on their skin. Dewdrops fell from the trees. The mist slowly evaporated as the sun rose. Some people closed their eyes against the sun. The group dispersed.

"Remember our Bapak!" someone shouted.

"There are no more memories!"

"There is no more past!"

"There is no future!"

"There is only the present!"

"That is absolute!"

They competed with the sun, the birds, the wind.

"We must be happy!"

"Until the time when we are no more!"

"Until there is no time for us!"

"No one may complain!"

"Or complain forever!"

"It all means the same thing to us!"

They stopped talking. The sun grew hotter and slowly chased the mountain chill away. The green of the trees shimmered in the sunlight.

Someone stopped suddenly and shouted, "Where's Pak Jaga, the night watchman?"

Alarmed, they looked around. He wasn't with them.

"He's not here!"

"I was just talking to him."

"What did he say?"

"He said that we must make a decision!"

A roar rippled through the crowd. Fearful shadows slithered through the group of women. They stepped aside to let the men scatter in every direction, searching through the grass, the flowers, the hillocks.

From the top of one knoll, a man shouted, "Look!"

People ran in the direction the man was pointing, squinting against the glare of the sun. A river of sparkling water, a mountain river, flowed swiftly between boulders. There, floating in the water between the rocks, was a body.

"Pak Jaga! Pak Jaga!"

It was the old night watchman. The women screamed. They quickly clambered down the slope and headed for the river. The women wept and shouted until the market groundskeeper scolded them.

"Be quiet! There's no use in crying! He chose to do this. It's stupid to cry over someone else's decision. Don't be fools! Your tears are useless!"

The women quieted down. Although they did not understand what he meant and their eyes opened wide in amazement, they stopped wailing.

"Your crying is a waste of time," said the groundskeeper, and he left them to descend to the river.

The river ran far below. It was a steep ravine and they had to be very careful. The men passed through the undergrowth, then disappeared behind the trees. The women stared after them. Then they remembered the market and their merchandise. When they had lost sight of the men, the women decided that they should return to the market.

The men stood at the edge of the river. They saw a figure in the water, stuck between some boulders. They looked up at the top of the slope and they realized that the night watchman had jumped from there.

"His courage!" said someone.

"His cowardice!" said someone else.

"There is no longer any meaning."

"It's all just the same."

"What's important now is that Pak Jaga is gone."

"Without any signs, without any explanation!"

Pak Jaga was sprawled out there on the rocks. The men standing at the river's edge were stunned at what had just happened. They gazed at the corpse for a long time as if they were examining their own lives. The sun's rays skimmed over the water, making it sparkle. Clear water splashed over the rocks. The mist had evaporated and the ravine was clear. Birds flying above headed for the rice fields.

"Shouldn't we get started?"

"Come on!"

They gingerly waded into the cold river water. The river splashed their clothes but they pushed forward, struggling through the water and carefully jumping from boulder to boulder. Ah, Pak Jaga!

"Courageous one!"

"Perfect freedom!"

"Every person, his own time and place!"

"Freedom to choose! To be or not to be!"

"It's the same for us!"

They crossed the river. Water, boulders, sky, sun. Trees and grass on the slopes. Open sky, sprawled corpse.

"Ah, the blood!"

"Ah, his smile!"

"Ah, the damage!"

"Ah, his handsome face!"

"There is no longer any sign of his age!"

They stood there staring at the corpse for a long time, musing, reflecting.

The women quickly returned to the bustle of the marketplace—engines roaring in the bus station, the smell of cabbages mixed with the odor of gasoline, steam rising off the hot asphalt streets. Just as it always had been, this was life in the market, even though there had been a change in the actors. Did this mean something?

As always, vegetables were taken from the mountain to the city every morning. The trucks were loaded at the market, and a chain of hands relayed the vegetables to kitchens in the city. A truck full of vegetables, people shouting, dogs roaming about freely. Customers in the market moved from stall to stall. They ate at crowded food stands that served steaming hot rice dishes. But, except for the women who had returned from the mountain that morning, none of them knew that they would never again see the old night watchman with the wrinkled sarong sleepily sipping tea at a food stall. Pak Jaga had left them to perfect his life.

Here is what happened at the market.

The sun beat down on their backs whenever they ventured out from under the shelter of the trees and market stalls. Traces of the mountain air and morning freshness could be found in the market under the trees, in the stalls, sheltered spots, and near the piles of vegetables. The market became crowded with more and more vendors and customers. Who could hear the alarm? An alarm was sounded in the midst of the market! All activity stopped immediately. Everyone looked around to see where the sound was coming from. A man with a paper funnel held at his mouth and a wooden knocker in his hand stood in the middle of the market. It was the market groundskeeper. The vendors left their stalls. What was the matter? The groundskeeper held up his loudspeaker.

"Friends! Pak Jaga had died!"

People poured out from the market stalls to gather around the man. The women who had arrived first and already knew the news waited quietly by their merchandise. They no longer cared about death. It was normal; it was a part of life. They resented the groundskeeper. He was the one who had ordered them to stop crying at the river and now, after they had accepted it, he announced the death in the middle of the market. The people who surrounded the groundskeeper asked: When did he die? Where? Why? When is the burial?

The groundskeeper shouted, "He committed suicide!"

Everyone gasped.

"He jumped from that peak," he said, "into the ravine!"

"Into the ravine?"

People pushed forward. The news had reached the food stalls outside the market.

"Did the body float away?"

"They said it was his own decision."

"His conscious decision."

"Is that so!"

"Indeed!"

"He committed suicide?"

"He ended his life."

They talked about the death. After a while, they left the gentle old groundskeeper to his thoughts. He tried to imagine the terror of throwing oneself from a peak into a ravine. That old man had killed himself. Why kill yourself when you are going to die in a little while anyway?

"He did it intentionally," someone said.

"Was he crazy?"

"Not at all."

"So how can it be true?"

"It is true. It's the truth!"

A ceremony of disappointment and sorrow silenced the market. People exchanged condolences. The groundskeeper disappeared. Several people searched for him and they finally found him lost in thought in a corner of the market.

"Where is the body now?" they asked.

The groundskeeper looked at them vacantly. He was confused. He surveyed the people surrounding him and then he stood up.

"His friends want to take the body to the sea. They're dragging the body down the river so that it will float away."

Then he was silent, his eyes reddened. The people who had gathered around him looked at each other, agitated. The groundskeeper moved away from the group. They let him go, but they disagreed with the treatment of the night watchman's body.

"This can't happen!"

"It's inhumane!"

"Curse them!"

"Let's chase after them!"

"He must be buried!"

They ran out of the market and the men started to shout. People poured out of the food stalls to see what the commotion was about.

"This is inhumane!"

They swore and cursed. The group grew larger after they left the market. Their curses could be heard reverberating down the road. Everyone who heard them joined the crowd. It became the longest procession in the history of the mountain.

But they did not find anything. Perhaps the corpse was badly damaged or eaten by vultures or had drifted away. No one knew. The secret was just a tiny tuck in the grand secret of life.

And the groundskeeper? He hid all day in the market office.

He told the market fee collector, "Know this: life ends with death! Do not be saddened by death. You will meet it eventually, perhaps intentionally, perhaps not. Life is a long fruitless journey! Emptiness is eternal! This is our heaviest burden!" When it was time to close the office, he refused to leave.

That evening, when the market was deserted, the office door opened to reveal the groundskeeper's sorrowful face. Deep-set eyes, wrinkled forehead and pale skin. He left the office and walked towards a truck that was about to leave the market. He ran, hoping to go somewhere where no one knew him. He left the market, hurling himself into a bigger life, without a name.

"This is my death before my life is over," he said to the truck driver's assistant.

The assistant let him hitch a ride. He asked the old man where he wanted to go.

The groundskeeper replied, "To a grander life!"

A life of misery is beyond comprehension.

Biographical Information

KUNTOWIJOYO was born in Bantul, Yogyakarta, in 1943. He learned to read the Koran when he attended elementary school at Ibtidaiyah Madrasah, and became a voracious reader of Indonesian literature in middle school. During his high school years in Surakarta, he began to read world literature and write his own short stories, essays, and plays.

While attending Universitas Gadjah Mada (UGM) in Yogyakarta, he founded the Lembaga Kebudayaan Seniman Islam (Islamic Artists Cultural Institution) and a literary study group, Mantika, along with other noted literary figures, including Ikranagara, Arifin C. Noer, Dawan Rahardjo, and Chaerul Umam. He graduated from UGM in 1969 with an undergraduate degree in history.

Kuntowijoyo earned his Master of Arts in American history from Connecticut University (1974) and his PhD in history from Columbia University in 1980. His doctoral dissertation was entitled "Social Change in an Agrarian Society: Madura 1850-1940." Upon returning to Indonesia to resume teaching at UGM, he founded the Center for Policy Research and Study with Amien Rais and Chairil Anwar, and he was active in Muhammadiyah, one of the largest Muslim social organizations in Indonesia. In addition to producing historical studies and essays, he also continued to write and publish short stories, poetry, and novels, many of which touched on aspects of Islam and Javanese culture.

In 1991, he suffered an attack of meningoencephalitis, but continued to write short stories and poetry. He died in February 2005.

Kuntowijoyo received numerous awards, including the Art Award from the Regional Government of Yogyakarta (1986), Literary Writing Award from the Centre for Language Advocacy and Development (1994), Culture Award from the Indonesian Association of Muslim Intellectuals (19995), Satyalencana Kebudayaan from the Government of Indonesia (1997), Mizan Award (1998), and the Southeast Asian Writers Award from the Government of Thailand (1999).

JOAN SUYENAGA was born and raised in Honolulu, Hawaii, and earned an MA in anthropology from the University of Hawaii. She began studying traditional Javanese gamelan music and language in the early 1970s, and has lived, raised a family, and worked in Yogyakarta as a freelance writer, translator, and editor, focusing on Indonesian and Javanese culture, for over 30 years.